Uptown L. ...

Secrets of an Usherette

by Marie Bryan

In loving memory

To my dad, my brother Chris and my friend Julie

Acknowledgement:

I would like to thank the following people for their help in the writing of this book:

My Mum who encouraged me and led the way in writing.

Kevin, for giving me the confidence and encouragement to start writing again.

Olivier, for making me believe I could publish my work and for supporting and educating me through the whole process.

My sister-in-law Claire, for taking the time out to read, re-read and edit my book.

Itumeleng for taking the time out to proofread and correct my grammar.

My daughter Korie for giving me all the constructive feedback.

My son AJ, I love you.

My darling Roy, I love you. Thankyou for all your love and support.

About the publisher

Voice Hub Publishing's aim is to give a voice to those who never had an opportunity to do so.

In this book Marie Bryan, tells us a story which took almost 25 years to complete.

A really hypnotic story of fictional characters sharing the same workplace each having a very poignant background story.

We hope that it will be the first of many more as we thoroughly enjoyed it.

Olivier Etienne, founder of Voice Hub Publishing, also did the illustration throughout the Book.

Sit back, relax and enjoy!!!

Disclaimer:

This is a work of fiction. Unless otherwise indicated, all the names, characters, businesses, places, events and incidents in this book are either the product of the author's imagination or used in a fictitious manner. Any resemblance to actual persons, living or dead, or actual events is purely coincidental.

Table of content:

Prologue

As Reama sat in the dressing room waiting to be announced to all the waiting fans; she wondered again as to the level of accomplishment she had achieved in such a short time. Reama had gained relative success over the years and was doing well. She had written five bestsellers, and each had been in the top ten. She had toured the world promoting her books and had gained a good legion of fans.

Her publishers had been surprised at her latest book as it had been different to the style of writing they were used to but Reama had insisted and had argued this was important to her. In the end they had given in, but were not confident it would do as well as the others. Their doubts had been proven wrong; it became her biggest bestseller to date.

Reama checked herself in the mirror and re-applied some more lipstick. She had kept in shape over the years and knew she still looked good. Her breasts were on view but not too much and she had carefully chosen her outfit which complimented her figure perfectly. She had styled her hair up and had worn pear drop diamante earrings which matched the choker she had on.

Reama was just adding the finishing touches to her make up, when the young assistant came into the room to announce they were ready for her. Her life was so different now than it was back then. She was no longer the young cinema usherette with dreams of making it into the big time. She was actually living that dream, or almost. There was just one last piece of the puzzle that would make it oh so perfect. She suddenly became nervous and anxious at the idea of whether he would be here tonight. How would he react towards her? Was he happy with his life? Her heart still flipped at the thought of him.

She took one more look in the mirror and smiled to herself. Again, she wondered how she had got to this moment…

Chapter 1: Reama

From as far back as she can remember; Reama wanted to be a writer. She had started reading from a young age and from then she had been eager to write. Reama loved to read stories in every form that she could find. Books, comics, movies, articles and even music. By the time she was eight, she had read all the books given to her. In the end her school did not know what to do with her. Her teacher purchased a thick Brothers Grimm book with all her favourite stories such as Cinderella, Sleeping Beauty, Rumpelstiltskin, Rapunzel, Hansel and Gretel, Snow White to name but a few.

Reama had loved and treasured this book and as a natural born escapist, she had spent every waking moment reading and re-reading this; as well as preferring to dream things up in her mind rather than play outside.

When she was in junior school, her teachers quickly picked up on her writing ability and encouraged her to write stories for school plays. One of her greatest achievements had been when she was asked to write the Christmas play one year. It had been a musical rendition of Mary and Joseph with a very modern take and twist to it. It had been a popular play and everyone had loved it. Reama had also entered a writing competition and she was one of twenty children locally whose stories had been published. This had been another of her greatest achievements. Her parents had been so proud they purchased ten copies to give to friends and family. They had encased the book they purchased; which held a place of pride in their cabinet.

As Reama got older, she felt like she had something important to say. She had written for the school paper and had become their editor. She had written anything from who had won the latest Football tournament to political debates about how better the food should be in the school canteen. She also became a member of a local writers club.

Reama felt that her writing had provided her with an outlet and she had discovered that writing and spreading her message was a major cause in her life; something that could help others if she were to promote it properly and one that could guide the reader to ultimately discover their own purpose.

Reama especially enjoyed writing about people and their lives, their dreams, aspirations, wants and desires and she loved to watch people. It was the chapter later in her life that would change everything and ultimately lead to the biggest selling book for her to date.

Her father did not share her enthusiasm for writing, but her mother did. As a young girl her mother had introduced her to books of a romantic kind, and they had shared a love of Mills and Boons! Her mother had left school at fifteen with no qualifications as she had to help care for her younger siblings. She had met Reama's father at nineteen and they had quickly got married.

It was not until she was in her fifties, that she summoned up the courage to enrol at the local college to complete her qualifications and it was there that she had developed a love of writing herself. She later attended a writing club where she had written short stories and Reama had been the one to read and edit these for her. She was so proud of her mother's achievements.

Her father, however, believed writing stories was a waste of time and that you either went to work or studied to become a teacher, a doctor or a solicitor. He had not been impressed when her mother had enrolled at college but knew better than to make his feelings known. Afterall he knew she had been a kind, loving wife who took care of them all and he loved her.

After school, Reama had gone to college to complete her A Levels. She had enrolled into a University course in Sheffield but did not quite like this and after the first year she decided to take a year out. She remembered that her parents had been so angry with her as they had hoped she would go on to be a teacher. Reama did not want to do this as writing was in her blood and she was determined to become a writer.

Reama's two older sisters had not been bothered with going to University. Instead, both settled for jobs they were relatively happy in. Her brothers had worked as apprentices and had secured their jobs through that. She had tried to explain to her parents but they would not listen. They had said that if she was to leave University and move back home she had to find a job. Reama felt she had no choice, so she moved back home and began to apply for jobs. She was not successful with any of them so in the meantime she enrolled onto a writing course at the local college. She had been in town one Friday afternoon looking for jobs and had been walking past Uptown Cinema; when she spotted a card on the glass in the Kiosk Booth advertising for staff. Feeling that she had no choice, Reama went to enquire about this.

Reama had never been to this Cinema before; preferring the one closest to where she lived. Besides, coming from a strict family background; she was not permitted to come into the Town Centre.

Inside the Kiosk Booth was sat a young girl of about twenty two years of age with a very thin face, slanted eyes and shoulder length mousy brown hair, who asked if she needed a ticket. Reama said no; but that she wanted to speak with someone about their vacancies. The young girl looked Reama up and down quickly, before saying she would need to speak to the manager on duty and pointed into the direction she needed to go.

As Reama walked up the steps, she entered into a grand looking foyer with a sea of red velvet carpet running on for what seemed like forever. Most of all was the smell that greeted her as she walked in. It was a mixture of sweet popcorn, hot dogs and coffee. She asked where the office was and was pointed up the grand staircase, where she was greeted by a woman in her early forties with shoulder length black hair streaked with grey.

Reama explained that she had come about the vacancies and was asked to complete a short mathematical test; which she passed easily and the job was hers. After that, it was explained what hours she would be expected to work and was guided into a nearby room where she was promptly fitted for a uniform and given a timetable of her working hours. Reama felt a growing excitement and couldn't wait to start her first shift.

Chapter 2: The Beginning

Reama started her first official shift the following Saturday. She had initially agreed to work part time as she was also at College. Reama wanted to be a writer and become a bestselling novelist and nothing was ever going to change that. In the meantime, she needed to earn some extra money and Uptown Cinema was as good a place as any.

Uptown Cinema had opened up in December 1933 housing over 2,500 seats with a fancy restaurant. Changes in ownership in 1944 resulted in the name change to Uptown. It originally had two screens which later changed in 1973 to three screens, with screens four and five opening in 1976, and finally screen six in 1988. To Reama, it was an enormous but exciting place to work in.

It had been arranged for Reama to meet the floor supervisor Sylvia; who would be the one to show her around and to explain what her job role would be. Reama soon found out she would be working as an Usherette and was given a black and bright orange torch. It would be a year later before she would work behind the Kiosk and the bar. The moment Reama had met Sylvia she did not like her. Sylvia had glided into the building or "floated in on her broomstick", others would say and had walked almost on tip toe to where the girls had been standing.

Sylvia was tall, but Reama remembered she was very bony and had dyed black hair that was brushed out into an almost afro style. The make-up she wore made her look like Bette Davis in her role from the film 'What ever happened to Baby Jane' and she looked very scary indeed. When she spoke, she was rude and abrupt with everyone and had spoken to Reama like she was a little child.

Sylvia had shown her around and had explained that her role as an usherette would be to take the tickets from the customers. She should tear them on the line and give the other half back to them then direct them to the relevant screen and seats. She was shown where she would put the other half of the tickets and where she would keep her torch.

During the matinee performances, Sylvia had explained to Reama that she would also be selling ice creams and ice lollies and had shown her around the Freezer room where Reama had first met Edna. Reama liked Edna immediately; who in contrast to Sylvia was much nicer, kinder and friendlier. Edna was a lot older than her but despite this, they struck up a friendship with Reama becoming very protective of her. Edna had calmly explained what she needed to do, shown her the ice cream trays she would be wearing to sell from and had given her a price list. It was expected that she priced things up in her head as calculators were forbidden; so she needed to memorise prices as quickly as possible.

Afterwards, Sylvia had taken Reama back upstairs and had introduced her to the other girls who were on shift. They included Sue and Tracey who were similar in age to Reama and they hit it off immediately. She went to meet Brenda, who worked in the kiosk and she had met the doormen on duty, as well as the projectionists. There had been a lot of names to remember but by the end of her shift she had remembered the majority of people's names.

Elaine had come in on a later shift. She had walked up to Reama and introduced herself then had asked her how her first day had been. It was a bold move, but Reama liked that and had been happy to answer her questions. It had been a long and very busy day and Reama quickly realised that Saturdays would be their busiest days followed by Sundays. A new blockbuster film had just been released and had come into the cinema two days previously.

A long queue of eager customers had formed outside, waiting for the late afternoon performance. The queue had gone all the way up the road and around the corner. Reama realised she had been significantly thrown into the deep end, plus she could see Sylvia out of the corner of her eye scrutinising her every move. Sylvia had really given Reama the creeps and she knew that Sylvia would not be a person to mess with.

As this was a full performance, Reama and the other usherettes had to go into the theatre to help seat the customers. As people came in; couples, groups of people and the odd singletons, Reama's job was to ask people to move along the aisles in order to free up seats for others. Reama found that most of the customers were obliging and happy to do this but others less so and reluctant to get up and move along. Reama felt out of her comfort zone as she had never had to deal with the general public before. She felt she lacked the confidence to challenge the less obliging ones. For those that confronted her, Tracey had stepped in to deal with it. Reama watched as Tracey engaged with the customer calmly and confidently. At one point, she had told one of them that if they continued to talk to her in that manner, she would have to ask him to leave and that they would be escorted out of the building by one of the doormen. The customer backed down before begrudgingly moving seats.

Once seated, Reama and the others had to check all the exits to make sure they were locked. Sue explained that often the kids opened the exits for their friends to get in; even some of the adults did this too. Sometimes some of them would even sneak into some of the other Theatres. This action would signal a comedy of errors with both doormen and usherettes chasing young people across the stage and up the different aisles before collaring one or two of them or before them getting away altogether.

Reama was also shocked to hear the girls tell her that on the odd occasions, they had witnessed women giving their dates blow jobs and them having to shine their torch on them then asking them to stop and leave. The girls were cracking up laughing at this but Reama could not believe what she was hearing and secretly hoped that she would not find herself in such an embarrassing position. She shuddered at the thought. As it turned out, Reama was to find herself mostly on shift with Elaine, Sue and Tracey and they had quickly become firm friends.

Reama soon learned that her job consisted of greeting the array of customers who frequented the cinema to come and watch the latest films. She collected, counted and recorded ticket sales, showed customers to their seats, where to find the nearest exit, bathrooms and concession stands, tried to answer various questions, ensuring they adhered to the safety rules. She also had to ensure that the front lobby was clean and tidy at all times, gathered and answered complaints or suggestions as well as selling ice cream during intervals. It was a busy job and Reama loved it. She had met the Manager Mrs Cross, who was a kind woman in her late fifties, as well as the General Manager; a man called Mr Langley. He was easy to get on with and was quite a funny man.

Mr Langley was a portly little man, standing at five foot five with a short fat neck, a big round stomach and balding hair; which he would comb over to give a full head of hair appearance. He had round hazel eyes which sat below thick greying eyebrows which were quite soft. He had a good sense of humour and would often joke that the reason why his stomach was so fat was because it held half a brewery's contents. It was rumoured that Mr Langley liked to drink and could often be found at the local pub drunk. Reama guessed that the rumours were true as his face often looked red, bloated and puffy and his nose a bulbous red.

He had been the General Manager for the last ten years. He was strict but fair with his staff, but god help you if you were unlucky to get on the wrong side of him. Staff always knew they were in trouble when he called you into his office. Once in he would slowly draw the curtains so no one could see into his office, but you could hear the distinctive roar of his voice when yelling at someone for some mistake they made. Despite all this, Reama had taken a liking to him.

Reama worked mostly on Friday evenings and all day Saturday and Sunday but during the holidays she would work additional days. She loved the hustle and bustle of cinema life and she had formed a close bond with some of the staff there. When she had been brash on her first day, Reama had initially been wary of Elaine. There was something about her she could not quite put her finger on, but over time she had got to know her better and learned a little more about her and her earlier life. However, despite this, Reama still could not help feeling that all was not what it seemed with Elaine. Elaine prided herself on the way she looked and dressed and she was obsessed with her weight, always watching what she was eating and talking about trying the latest fad diet. Reama also knew something else was going on as on a few occasions she had overheard

Elaine making herself sick in the staff toilets but had kept this to herself.

Reama enjoyed nights out with some of the girls particularly Sue and Tracey who loved to drink and party. Reama was aware that Sue and Tracey house shared and at times after a hard night of drinking, she would crash back at their place. She particularly liked Tracey and admired the way she had fought to get out of the life that she had come from but noted that she was obsessively clean.

Sue had also told Reama about the way in which Tracey and her family had lived and the state of the home conditions. Reama could not imagine living like that. She had come from a family of five and was the middle child, having two older sisters and two younger brothers. She had got on well with her siblings as well as her parents who were strict devout Catholics who had acted like drill sergeants when it came to keeping the house clean.

Each sibling was allocated a chore which they had to complete before they were able to watch TV or go out with friends. Beds had to be made and rooms hoovered or swept. Reama and her sisters took it in weekly turns to clean the kitchen, including the oven, wall, floor tiles and all the skirting boards. The bottle of bleach was the key cleaning instrument which held its pride of place under the kitchen sink and was used for everything from cleaning out the toilets to bleaching out the cups. Reama had felt extremely lucky after Sue told her about Tracey.

Chapter 3: Anton

Reama remembered the first time she had ever met Anton as if it was yesterday. The previous doorman Ronnie eventually retired having worked twenty years plus as he felt he needed a well-earned break. It was a cold autumn day and as always, the steady crowds were streaming in and out of the different theatres. It was about four pm when he walked in. Reama had been talking to a girl called Jessie who had been working on the kiosk and they were giggling about the antics of Friday Night when they had gone out to the local night club and Jessie had gone off with some guy she had met.

Anton had strutted through those huge doors like a supermodel, with his head held high and with an air of confidence and almost arrogance about him which she had never seen before. He had looked so confident and self-assured when he had walked up to them and introduced himself as if he was invited into their conversation. He was about six foot four inches tall, with a slim build and black wavy hair which fell just above his shoulders but it was his eyes that Reama had noticed the most. They were Hazel in colour; a combination of green, gold, and brown colouring which had set them apart from any other eyes she had ever seen. They were simply magnificent, making Anton look all the more mysterious and enchanting. In short, Anton was simply gorgeous! Jessie and Reama exchanged quick glances at each other before Reama told him where he needed to report to. As he was walking off, he caught the admiring glances of every female (staff and customers) he had walked past.

As Anton walked towards the staff room, he had actually been feeling scared and nervous as hell. He knew he was a little late, but he had to sort out his mum before he left which resulted in him missing the bus. He had been looking forward to working at Uptown Cinema as he had heard there were some nice girls working there. Plus he needed the extra money to save for a new car and his first holiday.

His mind drifted back briefly to the two girls he had met on the way in and wondered about one in particular he had just seen. He didn't know why, but he felt his heart flip over at the sight of her before quickly dismissing this. He was in a relationship, very happy and that is how it was going to stay.

Anton's mind wandered to his girlfriend Isabelle who he had met about six months ago on a night out with friends. She had been out with a bunch of friends from work and they had hit it off straight away and ended up talking the whole night. Isabelle was a pretty petite brunette with brown eyes and she seemed to have her head screwed on and was decent enough, but he recognised that there had been no instant passion.

Despite this he had been seeing her ever since and things were ticking along nicely. Plus his mum really liked her and felt she was good for him. Isabelle was twenty four years old to his twenty two and she was already talking about settling down and getting married. Anton wanted to please his mum so, if she was happy then he would be too. Anton's mum meant the world to him and he vowed to take care of her no matter what. She had been diagnosed with multiple sclerosis and his dad had left shortly after the diagnosis. They had twenty years of apparent happiness but then he just upped and left when she had needed him the most. He remembered that day well. He had tried to plead with his dad to stay but it was clear he had already made up his mind. Anton had not spoken to his dad since which was over a year and a half ago. He later heard rumours that his dad had been having an affair with a woman at his workplace and had moved in with her. His mum's illness had started to deteriorate after that and she was having problems with her vision, leg movements and balance. He admired her fight and her determination not to give into such an awful disease. Anton had even gone to the library to read up as much as he could about this, so he knew what he would be dealing with.

Before his dad left, Anton believed he had a pretty good life. His parents always seemed loving and attentive towards each other and he had memories of a happy childhood, spending holidays in the family caravan by the coast or going fishing and cricket matches with his dad. He used to wonder why his parents never had any more children and later learned that his mum had suffered a series of miscarriages before and after he was born. In the end they stopped trying and concentrated their efforts on him. In some respects, he was a spoiled child who pretty much always got what he wanted, something he had often used to his advantage. Anton liked to get what he wanted. Anton loved and worshipped his dad which was why it was so devastating when he left. His dad had tried to reach out to him since leaving, but Anton was just not ready to speak with him.

Anton had to walk through one of the main cinemas on the left to get to the back and climb stairs to the second floor to reach the staff room. When he got there he was greeted by a man who would be his supervisor. He was given his uniform to wear which was a blue matching trousers and jacket suit with a yellow shirt and matching blue tie. Anton was not impressed with what he saw but knew he would still look good in this. He was allocated a locker so he put his bag in there and went off to get changed. When he came back, he looked at himself in the mirror which was on the back of the wall and admitted he was certainly a handsome man who looked good. He had been right, he did look good in his uniform!

Anton revelled in being tall and even liked his lean build although he felt he could benefit from a few muscles in his stomach and arms. He had bronze skin and was lucky to be able to tan quite quickly at the first sign of sunshine. He had clear skin and a set square jaw that had a slight indent in his chin. He took out his brush and went over his hair once again. He was glad he had made the decision to grow it long and felt it suited him well. His hair was thick and naturally wavy and fell automatically to one side of his face. It had been mentioned to him over the years that he had the looks for modelling, but this was not something he was ever interested in.

All his life he wanted to be a mechanical engineer. He loved the idea of analysing and solving mechanical devices or being able to design or redesign things. Most of all he wanted to develop a prototype of a certain type of device and be the first to test this. He was already on an engineering course at college and hoped this would eventually lead him on to university. Anton took one last look in the mirror before joining the others on the main floor.

Chapter 4: Sylvia

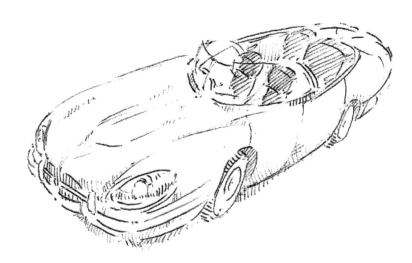

It had been a funny old day. Sylvia could not remember the last time that so many projectors had broken down all at once. Then the electrics had gone in the freezer room overnight causing all the ice cream to melt. It was a total mess. She wondered for the hundredth time whether it was time for her to retire. She did not have the time to deal with this type of crisis.

Sylvia assembled the staff together to go through the procedures. Having to deal with irate customers, giving their money back and offering complimentary tickets to appease the general public. In the hope they would forgive and come back to Uptown Cinema and not jump ship to the neighbouring rivals; only a few hundred yards away. As Sylvia gave out her instructions, she could not help but look at the young pretty girls in front of her and feel a pang of jealousy. Secretly, Sylvia thought that no matter how pretty the young girls in front of her were, none of them could compare to how beautiful she had been when she was their age. She had the world at her feet and a long line of handsome suitors chasing her.

Once again, Sylvia had despaired as to how life turned out for her. How had she ended up as floor supervisor working in a place that was so far removed from the world she had known.

Sylvia had been brought up in a tiny mining village. Her father worked all his life in the mines as did his father, grandfather and great grandfather before that. Sylvia's two older brothers had also worked in the mines. Sylvia was the only girl and the youngest child, and her parents had spoiled and doted on her. As Sylvia grew up, she began to tire of small Village life and had big dreams of moving to the City to make it big as a model. There was no doubt that Sylvia had been a stunner, standing at five foot nine with a slim frame, small waist and ample breasts. Sylvia had also been blessed with long black shiny wavy hair and dark brown eyes which seemed to smoulder. People often mistook her for a Gypsy and even compared her looks to that of Natalie Wood.

Sylvia had absolutely loved fashion and read every magazine she could. When rationing had ceased, the clothes that the average person wore were very different to those worn before the war. Whilst some women still wore corsets, the younger women favoured a more relaxed waistline. The fashion for young women's 'best dresses' was full-skirted dresses, with a stiffened petticoat underneath. Sylvia wore 'Pancake Make-up', which was applied with a damp sponge, and scarlet lipstick which was her favourite colour to wear and much to her parent's chagrin. Sylvia would sometimes wear trousers or 'slacks', but she had preferred the feminine look. Sylvia loved wearing high-heeled shoes and had hundreds of pairs in an array of colours. She loved her shoes and had imagined herself countless times walking down the catwalk at a Fashion show in Milan, Paris, New York and London. Oh, how she had craved the lure and seduction of the bright lights of the big City; she just could not wait to leave home.

Her parents had tried to stop her from going and even offered to pay for her to live close by. When Sylvia refused, her mother cried for months after she left but Sylvia had been determined. At age nineteen, she packed her bags and headed for the City.

When Sylvia arrived in the City, she landed herself a job at one of the big Department Stores in the perfume department. It had been a breeze. As soon as she went for the interview, she was offered the job on the spot. Sylvia also answered an advert for a house share where three other girls of a similar age were already living together. As soon as Sylvia met them, they hit it off immediately. The three girls, Gladys, Margaret and Doreen already worked in various secretarial jobs around the city.

Sylvia loved working at the Department Store. She wanted much more, still dreamed of becoming a model and she had started to save some of her wages to put a portfolio together. Sylvia had been more than confident that with her good looks and fantastic figure, she would secure top modelling jobs in no time.

Sylvia had been spending time looking through magazines and local papers to find a reputable photographer and one day whilst on her lunch break, one particular advert had caught her eye. Jonathon Nelson was a photographer who claimed not only to have taken photographs of some of the world's famous models but also to have photographed Royalty. It was this which had caught Sylvia's eye. She wrote the number down, called through and made an appointment for the following week. This was the beginning of her dreams.

The studio was situated in a back-street alley way which was just off the local High Street from where she was living. It was not very well lit and if you blinked you could have easily missed it. She ventured down the alley way then went through some large metal doors where she had to climb some stairs to the third floor as the lift had not been working. When Sylvia entered the room, the studio was not how she had imagined it would be. It was very small with a few pictures scattered around the walls of models. She noticed that there was a brown leather couch to one corner of the room which looked like it had seen better days. In the middle of the small room she saw what looked like a range of different camera equipment. There was a large camera on a tripod which stood in front of a wall which had a white screen behind it and on the floor were 2 smaller ones. For a moment Sylvia started to get a bad feeling about being there but quickly shrugged this off as Jonathon Nelson walked into the room. He was a man of fifty five years old who was short, about five foot six with balding hair and a staunch stomach. To Sylvia this man in front of her did not look like a photographer at all and he was not what she was expecting.

Jonathon Nelson beckoned Sylvia towards him and when she came forward he looked her up and down without saying a word.

'Did you bring a swimming suit with you?'

'Err yes I did'

'I need you to change into it please'

'Where's the changing room?' Sylvia asked.

'Changing room? There is no changing room here darling. If you want to be a model you better start getting rid of your shyness, it will not work in this business, you can change right here!!'

Sylvia started to feel a tingling of fear but tried to swallow this down. She told herself that he was right; if she was to become a model, she could not afford to be shy, so she started to take her clothes off. When she had stripped down to her underwear, Jonathon Nelson asked her to stop then just stared at her which felt like an eternity. Then out of nowhere he walked towards her, reached out his hand and began to fondle her breasts. Sylvia felt a fear she had never known grip her and she just froze. Jonathon's breathing changed, becoming slow and shallow, he started to groan as he reached down towards her pants. Sylvia did not know where she got the strength from, but she raised up her knee as hard as she could and kneed him in his groin. As he keeled over moaning in pain, Sylvia pushed him as hard as she could and he stumbled and fell backwards. Sylvia grabbed the rest of her clothes and ran out of the studio as fast as she could, taking the stairs two at a time. When she got out of the building she ran as fast as she could until she reached the end of the alley way back near to the High Street. She leaned against a post, bent over and started to throw up. She began to cry and it was a while before she realised she was still in her underwear.

Sylvia was brought abruptly back to the present by Sue who had been asking her what she should say to a customer who had been rude and offensive. Sylvia responded to her quite harshly but quickly regretted this. She liked Sue and knew she was being unfair, although she would never admit to this.

'And what do you expect me to do about it? Are you stupid or something?'

'He is insisting on talking to you'.

Sylvia became irritated as she followed Sue towards the customer.

'What seems to be the problem Sir?'

'Why can't we get any ice creams?'

Sylvia so wanted to give this man what for.

'I am so sorry Sir but there has been an electrical fault during the night which has caused the freezers to shut down damaging all the stock. We are rectifying the situation as best as we can and we are waiting for an emergency supply of stock. They should be here within the next hour. We are so very sorry for the inconvenience'.

'In the next hour you say?'

'Yes sir, we had to ring this through at short notice'.

'This isn't good enough'

'I understand that Sir but in the meantime there are still

other things you can purchase such as hot dogs, sweets, popcorn and drinks'.

Normally Sylvia would not feel this irritated but for some reason this customer was really winding her up. Maybe he reminded her of someone.

After the incident with the photographer, Sylvia had retreated into her shell and almost became a recluse. She refused to leave the flat which resulted in her losing her job at the Department Store. The other girls became worried about her and called a Doctor who said she was suffering from shock and had prescribed her some pills. Sylvia never told them or anyone else what happened, as she had felt too ashamed. How could she have been so stupid? So desperate? After what happened Sylvia knew she would never be so gullible again.

As time went by, Sylvia began to feel stronger in herself. She felt more confident and decided it was time to get another job, especially as the girls had been carrying her for long enough. She came across the advert for an usherette by chance. She had been using some newspapers to clean the windows when it had caught her eye. She read this and felt it sounded very interesting, especially as she used to go to the Cinema often when growing up. A new Movie Theatre had just opened in the City and they were looking for staff. Sylvia decided to apply for this.

When Sylvia had first arrived at The Ritz, she was greeted by a large illuminated vertical sign announcing the name of the place for the whole world to see. Even if the film showing was not that good the sign alone at the front had been enough to lure the customers inside. It was beautiful. Glamorous inside as it was on the outside. There had been something about the lush, heavy red, velvet curtains covering the screen at the back wall which gave the auditorium an aura of Majestic beauty which demanded that people wear their best clothes, show respect and be on their best behaviour. There was always a long queue to get in and there had been a Concierge whose job it was to stand in front to keep everyone in order. When he unhooked the thick white rope, everyone would file through to pay for their tickets at the square Kiosk in the middle.

The Ritz had red carpeted stairs the customers had to climb up by holding onto the gleaming brass bannister rails which would lead them to the dress circle. Here they would be greeted by an usherette to escort customers to their seats using a large orange torch as it was so dark. Everyone had been dressed in more finery than a decorated soldier. The men had worn burgundy trousers and a long jacket with gold epaulettes on each shoulder. They had worn matching peak caps which made them look like captains of a ship. The usherettes had worn the same colours but theirs had been a knee length pencil skirt, matching waist Jacket and also a pillbox hat perched on the top of their heads; which resembled the ones flight attendants used to wear.

Sylvia let out a heavy sigh. Things had certainly changed since then. Gone were the glamorous uniforms which made them look like models out of a magazine and in their place, there was the new uniform which left a lot to be desired. They were now forced to wear a blue A line skirt which was calf length with a matching boxed blue jacket, a yellow shirt and blue tie, no head wear. This new line of uniform somehow did not seem to fit into the Uptown cinema décor, but the Area Manager had made his decision, and this was what they had to endure. Everyone hated them including herself and they had all put up a fight except Edna who had never complained or made a comment like the others and had graciously done what she was told.

Sylvia loved working at the Ritz. It was glamorous, glitzy, exciting and infamous. Not only did the Ritz show the latest movies every week; after closing it would hold a 'men only' club. All types of gentleman from across the City with money to spend came to indulge themselves in games such as poker and Russian roulette. The men wore suits together with waistcoats, ties and white shirts. Sylvia had been fascinated as to how some of these men had worn their Trilby hats at an angle of approximately ten degrees from horizontal, which were common at the time. It had been so exciting and Sylvia and a few other girls had been especially chosen to keep these men afloat with cigarettes and an endless supply of alcohol.

It was here that she had met and had fallen instantly in love with Thomas Fletcher.

Thomas Fletcher had been about seven years older than Sylvia. He was six foot two inches, with a long tall muscular frame, blonde hair cut with a quiff at the front and the bluest eyes she had ever seen in her entire life. He was so handsome. He had come in one night with a group of friends and noticed her as quickly as she noticed him when he arrived. He had beckoned Sylvia over to him to order a round of drinks and cigarettes. When she returned with them, he asked her name and they started to talk and ended up talking the whole night.

Their relationship started very quickly. Thomas told 'Sylvie' as he liked to affectionately call her by, that he and his friends worked on the Stock Exchange and had been working there for a while. He owned a red little sports car and had an apartment one would only find in the pages of a magazine. Thomas certainly swept Sylvia off her feet. Within months, Thomas had encouraged Sylvia to give up her job and they got married. Life had been bliss and Sylvia had everything she could ever dream of. Even though she had not made it as a model, she made it as Mrs Fletcher, which was just as good. She had quickly immersed herself into 'High Society' life, going to the best restaurants and parties in town, wearing the latest fashionable clothes, and jewellery that would make Elizabeth Taylor herself jealous. She was definitely living the high life. It was all about to come crashing down around her.

Sylvia shuddered at the thought of how things had turned out, how blind and stupid she had become. She had been so busy living a charmed life, she failed to notice the warning signs in front of her and the changes in Thomas. Not at first anyway. She remembered that Thomas had been working longer hours and had been looking more and more tired and withdrawn. He had even started to comment on how much she had been spending, something he had never done before. Thomas had always insisted that she could have whatever she wanted no matter the cost.

One-night Thomas came home really late and had come into the bedroom to wake her up. She could tell that Thomas had been drinking and what startled her more was the fact that he looked like he had been crying so she started to feel scared. Thomas had slumped onto the side of the bed, sat there in total silence, his head down staring into the glass of brandy he was holding in his hand. As soon as he looked up at Sylvia, his face white and ashen, she knew that something was terribly wrong. Sylvia did not know what to do and spoke to him in a whisper, almost afraid someone would overhear what was to come.

'Thomas what's wrong?'

It seemed like a lifetime before he answered her.

'Something awful has happened,' he said. 'I've lost it all Sylvie, the whole damn lot!' Sylvia could still remember the shock she felt - she had absolutely no idea. Sylvia blinked and stared at Thomas in horror. Her hands trembled as she tried to make out what he just told her. Her heart was racing wildly and she felt breathless. She could not understand a word of Thomas's careful explanation of how he had lost everything. "How could it be that he had been so reckless?" the question screamed in her head. With tears pouring down her cheeks, she begged Thomas to find a solution to reverse this devastating situation.

'What do you mean Thomas?'

'We have no money left Sylvie, everything has gone'.

'What are you talking about Thomas? What do you mean

we have no money left?'

'I invested everything into a company which has gone bust. I even re-mortgaged the apartment to finance this. It's all gone love'. Then Thomas began to cry. Sylvia just sat there in complete and utter shock as she tried to digest what he had just told her. Broke? Lost it all? nothing left? As his words started to penetrate her mind and sink in, Sylvia began to feel the anger start to rage inside her. She jumped out of the large luxurious double bed they shared and started to pace their room. Sylvia loved this bedroom. It had been large with windows overlooking the whole of the city, which had views that went on for miles and miles. There would be some nights where she would sit in a window seat and just look out at the beautiful view before her, thankful for the life she had. All that would be gone now and it was down to Thomas.

'You stupid, stupid man, how could you? How could you Thomas?'. She was furious now and began yelling and shouting at him.

'Now what are we going to do?' Thomas had continued to cry and did not look at Sylvia once.

'I don't know Sylvie; I just don't know'.

She had not slept that night; neither of them did. They had talked long into the night until the rising of the early morning sun and they could hear the birds chirping in the trees. Thomas went on to explain that a business deal had gone dreadfully wrong. It was complex what had happened, but he explained the company had lost a great deal of money. Sylvia could hardly take in what he was saying. Thomas was always busy, and she never had any reason to discuss his business dealings with him. There had been no lead-up, no tell-tale signs that this was coming. From Thomas's face she could tell that he, too, was in total disbelief.

Though they did not know it at the time, it was to be the beginning of their nightmare that would eventually tear their lives apart. Over the next few days, the words kept reverberating through her head. "We have lost everything Sylvie." She tried to console herself that the worst might not happen. Thomas worked day and night to try to stave off the bankruptcy - but it was to no avail. Within months he lost the company he had so lovingly built up and was officially declared bankrupt. Sylvia and Thomas were totally unprepared for what was to come. She had no idea what happened during bankruptcy. It seemed as if, overnight, their lives changed completely. From being a company director, whose days were full of phone calls, conferences and lunches, Thomas was suddenly at home all day, lonely and rudderless. Unlike someone else who has lost their job, there was no redundancy money to fall back on. Indeed, as a bankrupt, Thomas was no longer allowed even to have a bank account.

A few weeks later, the cars were gone. Unknown to Sylvia they were bought on finance and had been repossessed. It was so shameful. It seemed she was losing everything that had given her the status she had so cherished. Having no choice, Sylvia had taken a job in a little dress shop and worked every spare hour to earn extra money to keep them afloat. Suddenly being without Thomas's substantial five-figure salary was a devastating blow. The bills came in as usual; the weekly shopping had to be bought. Her salary simply could not stretch to cover everything. So, she did what most people do when they do not have enough money to live on, they cut back drastically on their lifestyle and used credit to fund household bills.

Sylvia used to shop in designer boutiques but now she browsed second-hand shops, saving all the money she could and sold off many of her designer clothes. Gradually, their debts began mounting. Once, opening the mail had been an enjoyable breakfast ritual, but now the sound of the post on the mat made her heart thud with worry. She dreaded the phone ringing, too, in case it was a demand for money. Neither she nor Thomas could sleep properly. When she did sleep, she would wake up in the morning feeling sick and worn out. Some days Sylvia could not even eat - she had just lost her appetite. On her worst days, she would lock herself in the bathroom and sob for hours.

Their relationship began to suffer, too. She had vowed to stand by Thomas and was sure they could get through those difficult times and emerge a stronger couple. They tried to communicate, but it was always about money and the misery they found themselves in. They would sit and have serious talks for hours, going around and around the same old issues but not making any headway. They tried to keep life as normal as possible and still shared a bed. After a while they began drifting apart and the atmosphere in the house was incredibly tense. Money was obviously tight, and every day meant a financial juggle, but they lived like paupers and tried to eke out her salary to cover the bare essentials. Sylvia and Thomas were hardly speaking to one another and he was starting to spend more and more time away from home. When he was home, they did not even argue - there was just a tense silence between them. All the joy had gone out of their relationship. Their money worries had simply driven them apart.

At times looking back Sylvia still felt bitter as to what became of her life. She wished she had known more about Thomas's business and a shiver still ran through her whenever she thought about it. It was one of the most painful things she had ever had to go through, something that changed her life irrevocably.

Thomas continued to work here and there but eventually he left Sylvia for a rich socialite and she never saw him again. Sylvia was so heartbroken she packed up what little belongings she had left, took a train and stayed on it until it reached its final destination. She had not planned where she was going and did not care. She knew she was not going back home to her parents' house as she had not spoken to them in years and did not want to face them. She just wanted to be as far away from the City as possible. When the train had reached its terminus, Sylvia got off, found a local bed and breakfast and started to make plans for her new life. A few weeks later a job had been advertised for Uptown Cinema. Due to her experiences of working at the Ritz she was hired on the spot and had remained there ever since. Sylvia had found herself a small flat which was sparsely decorated and resolved to live a lonely life.

Chapter 5: Elaine

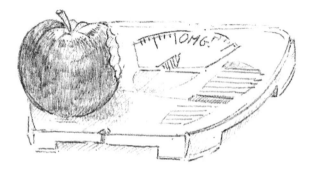

Elaine could not wait to get home from work. She had done a double shift as she was saving for a well-earned holiday. She hated the staff uniform and wondered again for the hundredth time who came up with such a poorly designed outfit? The skirt was a blue A line design which fell to just below the knees, a yellow polyester shirt, blue tie and a blue blazer, all of which hung off her slim delicate frame making it look two sizes too big for her!!.

She quickly undressed and placed her uniform on a coat hanger, before hanging it up in her wardrobe for her shift the next day. Whilst still in her pants and bra, Elaine went into the bathroom, leaned over the toilet, slid the pen she kept by the bowl into her throat and started to make herself sick. Tonight was the first time Elaine's stomach physically hurt from vomiting. She could feel her heart thump as she pushed the pen back and forwards, in and out of her throat. Elaine knew she could not keep doing this. She noticed that, as time went on, she no longer seemed to be as repulsed by her stomach contents as before. The chocolate mess she bought up was no longer unusual and disgusting to her but a symbol of her own failure and greed. The wrenching of her stomach caused the blood to rush to Elaine's head as she repeatedly regurgitated. After the mass of bread she had consumed earlier in the day at her lunch break, the food was difficult to get back up. Elaine had to drink glasses of water to get the food up, but this caused the sickness to be a bit like projectile vomiting and some of it had splashed onto the floor. After she had finished, she sat back on the floor feeling spent and thought to herself that tomorrow would be different. You will see.

Elaine thought back to the time all this started for her. She had returned home from school one day and she had found her 'Aunt' sitting on the sofa in the living room. She had come to visit from abroad and was planning to stay for a few days. Elaine did not really know this Aunt very well as she had only met her a few times over the years. Of course, she was not really her Aunt, but she was the sister of her Foster Mother Christine. The first thing her 'Aunt' noticed was that Elaine had gained weight since the last time she had seen her.

"My God Elaine, look how much weight you've put on?

Why are you not looking after yourself more?"

Elaine just stood there silent whilst her Aunt continued on.

"All that weight makes you look fat!"

Elaine knew she had put on some weight but did not think much of this. After all she was dealing with all the body changes that occur when you are a teenager. Elaine's foster brothers were constantly teasing and making fun of her because she looked chubby. Maybe it was not serious at all to them, but it was pretty painful for Elaine. They might have called her that just for fun. She would always feel horrible hearing them calling her those names.

Elaine's early childhood was spent in the foster care system. The first time she went into foster care she was five years old. Throughout her childhood and early years, Elaine had gone to five different foster homes before coming to Christine's at eleven years old. Elaine had a younger brother and sister who shared the same mother, but each had different fathers. There had been no one in Elaine's family who could offer her any care. That is how she ended up entering the care system. She had some memory of her mother but not much. Her social worker had said that her mother was unable to care for her as she was addicted to drugs and alcohol. Elaine's mother never really knew her father. It was believed he had likely been a paying customer when she had the need to go and make some money to feed her habit.

Elaine knew where her mother was currently living but had no interest in meeting her. Why would she? As she looked back at those years, it felt like a mixture of good and bad experiences for her. One of the most difficult parts of foster care for Elaine was not knowing what was going to happen to her next. There was always a sense of uncertainty and confusion and she often felt scared and alone. The only time that she really remembered her social worker was when she came to take her to the different places she ended up. Elaine could not remember a social worker ever talking with her or visiting her in her foster homes. It was important to her to know what was happening in her life. She needed someone to explain the situation to her in a way that she could understand. Someone she could trust and talk to about things.

Despite being in care, Elaine had grown to love her foster mother Christine. She was a woman in her late fifties with very short hair she used to dye burgundy. Christine was a small woman with a thin frame and greeny blue eyes. Christine had a kind face and a warm smile that made Elaine feel very welcomed and gave her a wonderful and nurturing foster home. Christine had shown Elaine love, patience, and kindness – all of the things a child needed. It felt like a real home to her. They each had household chores to do. Elaine learned about cleaning, cooking, laundry and budgeting. Christine took the time to listen and explain things to her in a way that Elaine could understand. She talked to her about her mum and why she could not take care of them. That was the first time Elaine remembered someone explaining the situation to her.

Being separated from her siblings was another painful part of being in foster care for Elaine. She was the oldest followed by her brother and baby sister. She could never understand why they were all placed in separate homes. At that time, most foster homes only wanted babies or very young children. Elaine always wondered about them and what they were doing.

Elaine remembered that at school all the girls seemed pretty to her and soon she thought she was in love. There was this boy in her year who was popular, good looking and charming as hell. She wanted to look slim for him so she ate as little as possible. Things had gotten so bad that she did not eat for more than ten days in a row, to the point where she would puke on an apple. Elaine had found it difficult to sleep and could not stand starvation. She switched to eating then making herself sick instead. She lost a lot of weight and still wanted to lose more.

Elaine was pretty tall at five foot eight inches and weighed about seven stone. Elaine remembered that after that the comments were about how thin she looked. She had been so upset about these comments because she had been proud of herself. Her bones felt comforting and she did not need anything other than getting thinner. People were never pleased with her body and she used to think back then, "my body is my business".

Things had gone too far back then. Elaine had started leaving home after meals to go to public toilets and puke until Christine had found out what she was doing and tried to stop her from doing it anymore. Christine was so worried about Elaine, she would take her house keys and force her to stay inside for at least four hours after having eaten. In response, Elaine would tremble, cry and scream, just like a drug addict. In the end Christine and social services had gotten her some help at a specialist residential unit. She would eat normally but would still have moments where she would think about making herself sick, but these were rare. When Elaine returned home, the doctors had said she was cured and everyone thought it was finally over. In some ways it was. After a month things had started all over again. Only this time she was more careful about this.

Elaine did not have many friends at school. Her eating disorder had put paid to that. She left school with very few qualifications and had drifted in and out of mundane jobs. Working at a Petrol station did not last long as it was difficult for her to go off to be sick. The same as a shop assistant and factory worker. She could not stay in a job very long as her secret had dictated this.

One day whilst flicking through the papers, she saw a job advertised for Uptown Cinema. She thought it would be something different and decided to apply. When she had gone for the interview, she had to do a maths test. Luckily it was basic maths which she passed. That was three years ago and she was still there; the longest job she had been in.

Elaine loved working at Uptown Cinema. She had made some friends, but she mostly enjoyed watching those movies where she could imagine herself as the lead with a gorgeous leading man beside her. How she would look slim with ample breasts feeling like the most beautiful woman in the world. At times it was very tiring, but the free movies made it worth it. It was very fast paced at times and so slow at others she would be bored to tears. She used to work at the box office and called it the "box of death". On weeknights, she was so bored, she wanted to pull her hair out. On weekends though, it would be so busy, there were times she could not take a break.

The next morning, the first thought that came to Elaine upon awakening, was what she did last night. She checked her stomach to make sure her pelvic bones were at the highest point and her stomach was concave. They were not, so she went into the bathroom and weighed herself. This would not be the first time Elaine would be stepping on the scales today. The morning was the most important weigh-in. This will be the lowest weight of the day and it would affect the course of the day. Some people read their horoscope, but Elaine read her weight scale. The number on the scale was in direct proportion to how she would feel for that day.

Elaine cleaned up the mess from last night. There were scrambled eggs spilled on the stove top, an empty cereal box sitting on the counter, and on the kitchen table she saw an empty carton of mint choc chip ice cream, an empty packet of crisp and empty cans of diet cola. As she started cleaning the stove top, she promised herself that today would be different. She was sick and tired of living life like this.

Elaine looked at the clock and saw that the cleaning took longer than she thought it would. Before she got into the shower, Elaine weighed herself again and checked her body in the full-length mirror at the back of the bathroom door. She felt disgusted. Her thighs were touching and her stomach looked like it was sticking out. Elaine tried to tell herself that it was that time of the month and that is what was wrong with her stomach, although she rarely had a monthly cycle these days. The doctor had told her that the lack of periods was because of her hormones being out of balance, but she had so many more symptoms. Her hair was getting thin, her nails were brittle, and her skin was looking so dry. Elaine felt tired all the time and there were times when she felt faint, especially after throwing up. Sometimes Elaine would feel so shaky it would be difficult for her to put her mascara on.

Elaine put on her makeup carefully, avoiding looking into her eyes. When she eventually summed up the courage to look into her eyes, she felt nothing but loathing and disgust. She hated herself so much. When not in the dreary work uniform, Elaine liked to dress impeccably. She had always tried to look pretty, and people would often tell her she was beautiful and compliment her on the shape of her brown eyes, but Elaine never believed them. If only they knew how she really felt.

Elaine felt anxious about getting to work on time. She looked up at the clock on the wall in the kitchen and saw that she was already late. On the way to work, she made up a story in her head to tell Sylvia about why she was late. She did not want to admit it, but she was also looking forward to seeing Anton. When she had first seen him, she had been instantly attracted to him and she made a promise to herself that she would lose enough weight for him to notice her.

When she arrived at work, she slipped into the staff room unnoticed. Someone had brought in a box of doughnuts, so she decided to have one. It tasted so good and Elaine savoured its sweetness. She tried to make it last, but the doughnut disappeared too fast. She decided to have another one trying to recapture that sensation she felt with the first bite. But it did not taste like that. Elaine kept thinking that the next bite would do the trick. The second doughnut disappeared faster than the first. What had she done? She would gain a lot of weight from eating two doughnuts. She must get rid of it. Elaine went into the bathroom but realised that someone else was in there too. She waited for them to leave. As they left someone else entered. She could not wait much longer so she went into a cubicle. Elaine believed that the calories were already dispersing into her fat cells and she had not even gone to sort out which cinema she would be in. Elaine vomited as she flushed the toilet hoping the noise would cover up the sound of her purging. She cleaned up and looked into her blurry red shot eyes. It looked like she had been crying and she had broken a blood vessel in her eye. Elaine checked herself one more time in the mirror and saw that her stomach looked bigger. She sighed and left the staff room.

Elaine was allocated to Cinema five at the bottom of the stairs. She was glad for this as it was quiet and isolated down there. When she arrived, she started looking for the eye drops in her jacket pocket. She kept looking then realised for a moment she had forgotten what she was looking for. She remembered, found the eye drops and then got back to work.

As Elaine waited to greet customers and take their tickets for the next performance, she thought about the doughnuts she ate earlier. Later on, that day she went into the staff room, the doughnuts were still there so she ate one doughnut, then another and another making sure no one saw her. Eventually, Sue came in and asked where the doughnuts were. Elaine had said that everyone must have liked them because she had just finished the last one. Elaine could not get to the bathroom soon enough before once again emptying her stomach.

At lunch times, Elaine preferred to eat alone but it was difficult at work. Sue, Tracey, Reama and the other girls were always wanting to go out somewhere to eat and she did not want anyone to see how much she ate. When going to lunch with them, she would usually end up eating quite a bit and then make herself sick afterwards. Sue and Tracey would often say things like "How do you stay so skinny eating so much?" then Elaine would tell herself that she would not eat with them again.

As Elaine got home, the phone rang. She ignored it, so the answering machine picked it up. Elaine hoped that they did not leave a message because then she would feel bad if she did not call them back. She just wanted to be left alone. The voice on the machine asks her where she was. She was supposed to have gone to counselling that evening. It was difficult for Elaine to make appointments with anyone because she never knew when she would be available and not busy with her eating disorder. Elaine went into her bathroom and weighed herself again before going to bed.

Chapter 6: Edna

Edna woke with a fright. She had that dream again. It was the third time this week. Edna could not understand why she was having this same dream and after all this time. She looked at the clock on her bedside cabinet that told her it was 5:30am. She could not get back to sleep so she got up, put on her glasses and went into the kitchen to make herself a cup of tea. She filled the kettle up with water and leaned back onto the counter waiting for it to boil.

She tried to figure out the meaning of this dream and what it was telling her. As Edna stood in the kitchen, one by one her cats came into the kitchen to see what was going on. As each one purred and nudged against her leg, Edna greeted each one as if they were her own children. They were all she had in the world really. Over the years she had developed a fondness for animals, cats in particular. She had initially taken in a stray ginger cat she called Molly and as time went on she took in more and more strays. They had become her babies, her family and Edna had loved and cared for every single one of them.

Edna had no family to speak of and had been an only child. Edna had known since childhood that she was born 'out of wedlock' . She had been born in a hostel for unmarried mothers after her father had deserted her Mother as soon as he discovered her mother was pregnant. Her mother never spoke about her father. Edna had a feeling she looked a lot like him as she did not resemble her mother at all who was the complete opposite of her in every way.

Standing at five foot two inches, Edna had brown auburn hair which was now tinted with grey. She wore her hair short above her ears. Her mother had blonde hair which she wore long to her shoulders. Edna had chocolate brown eyes which were round and frog-like, something she used to be teased for as a child whilst her mother had emerald-green eyes which looked exotic.

Since then her mother seemed to punish Edna for her own misgivings not ever knowing or understanding the humiliating ordeal her mother had gone through as a woman expecting a baby outside of marriage. Most of Edna's life was spent taking care of her mother whose overbearing ways and cutting tongue ensured that no one stayed around long enough to get to know her. Growing up, the stigma surrounding her conception and birth hung in the air like a bad smell and people were still unforgiving of this. This had kept them pretty much ostracised from the local community. It was unfair that she had to suffer on account of this but that was life; people were cruel. Edna did not particularly like her mother at times. Despite how she was, she loved her. She marvelled at a woman who could be so cruel . She wondered again what life had dealt her mother and why she became the way she did.

Edna sat at the table in the small kitchen, pondering about the dream that had startled her out of her sleep. After her mum died, Edna did not want to stay in the house they had shared. She had exchanged it for a small two-bedroom bungalow in a quiet area which sat neatly in the corner of a Cul-de-sac. This compact spacious home suited Edna who appreciated the quiet and solace that came with it. Her kitchen was simply decorated with white walls and the standard produced white council kitchen units with silver handles, chequered black and white lino on the floor; which housed the small table and two chairs.

Edna had not had that dream in such a long time; had not dreamt about him. Edna often wondered what it would have been like to have been married and had children of her own. She felt she would have been a good mother and would have given her children love and affection unlike her own mother.

There had been someone very special in her life and she loved and adored him but that was over thirty years ago. Ken Martin had been the sales assistant in the shop she went to to buy her groceries. He had been someone she had remembered from school but back then he had not really said that much to her. Every time she went in to do her shopping, Ken would greet her with a warm smile, a wink then would ask her how she was doing.

Edna knew she was not beautiful like some of the other girls and had envied their looks and figures and the glamorous way in which some of them dressed. Compared to them, Edna was plain. Her clothes looked shabby and dowdy which hung loose around her tiny frame. She never wore makeup and her hair was always pinned up in a bun sitting on the top of her head. Nevertheless, Ken Martin had noticed Edna and she had noticed him too.

Ken's friendly banter with Edna continued over the next few months until he plucked up the courage to ask her out on a date. Edna had gone in to do the usual weekly shop and she had been surprised and reluctant, scared as to what her mother would have to say about her going out with a man. She decided to take Ken up on his offer and not mention this to her mother; not yet anyhow.

Edna had arranged to meet Ken a few days later. Before leaving the house, she had made sure that her mother was fed and comfortable before slipping out to meet him. They ended up having a wonderful time together that evening. They had gone to the movie theatre to take in an old romantic film. Edna loved watching old Hollywood movies, especially ones with her favourite actresses such as Bette Davies, Rita Hayworth, Joan Crawford and Jayne Mansfield. These women always seemed to be tough and strong after being hurt by life. A bit like her in some ways but not as beautiful and glamorous! They had gone for a walk afterwards and had talked all evening.

It was the first time in Edna's life that she felt she was able to open up about her life, her parents and her feelings around this. Ken had been an attentive listener, taking time and patience with her allowing her to talk openly and freely. It had felt good and Edna knew there and then that she had fallen in love with Ken.

They continued seeing each other over the next few months; finding the time to spend as much time together as they could. Edna had still not yet told her mother about Ken and kept putting the inevitable off. If she was honest with herself, she was scared of what her mother would say. She had such a cold vicious tongue and Edna knew she could be cruel, make her feel like she was not worthy enough and Edna was not ready to hear that, not yet anyway. She felt incredibly happy and did not want that feeling to end.

A few weeks later, Ken left to attend a pre-arranged visit to his relatives up in the North East. As much as he did not want to go he could not get out of this. A cousin of his was getting married and had asked Ken to be his best man. Ken did ask Edna to go with him. This would have meant staying away for a couple of days and there would have been no one to care for her mother. Edna had yet to tell her about Ken. She had been devastated about this but knew she had put herself in this situation.

Edna had gone with Ken to the train station and he had promised her that when he returned, they would both go together to visit her mother as he wanted to marry her. Edna nearly burst with pride, she felt so happy she swore she had floated back home.

It had been over a week before Edna found out what had happened. Edna knew something was wrong when Ken did not arrive back at the train station. They had arranged for her to meet him off the train and the plan was to go straight to her mother's house. The scheduled train came in at 6pm and she had waited in eager anticipation for him to arrive. When she didn't see him, her heart sank immediately.

Nevertheless, Edna waited at that train station until the last train came in at 10:00pm. She had been sitting on an old tatty bench at the side of the station silently crying into her tissue.

Edna thought to herself that her Mum had been right. She wasn't worthy and she certainly wasn't worthy of any relationship. How could she have been so stupid? What man would really want to marry her? She believed that Ken had gone away and decided he did not want to be with her anymore. Rather than tell her face to face, he had taken the coward's way out and had avoided her. Edna had sat on that bench late into the night before getting up and slowly walking home. She entered the house quietly, tiptoed up the stairs and checked in on her mum who was snoring loudly. She was glad that she hadn't told her about Ken, the humiliation would have been unbearable. Edna went to her room, collapsed on her bed and cried herself to sleep.

About a week later Edna reluctantly went into the grocery store where Ken worked. Her mum had wanted some items and even though she tried to protest, her mum had been insistent. The second nearest shop was a few miles away plus what her mum wanted could only be bought from that store. With a heavy heart, she had left the house. She didn't know what he would say when she got there. Would he be there? Would he speak to her? She had felt so scared and nervous. When she got there she was relieved to see he wasn't there and wondered if he had even come back from his visit up North. Whilst waiting in the queue, she overheard some older ladies in front of her gossiping.

'I'm going to miss seeing Ken here. It's such a shame about him been stabbed like that'

'He was such a nice man. I heard he got into a fight at a stag do and someone stabbed him, died right there and then, poor man. It's true what they say, the good do die young'

Edna felt like her heart had stopped beating and for a moment she found it hard to breathe. Had she heard right?

'Excuse me, I didn't mean to listen in to your conversation, but which Ken are you talking about?

'No, you shouldn't be listening in to people's conversation, but if you must know we are talking about Ken Martin; who worked here for years. He went up to the North East

for his cousin's wedding and got stabbed on his cousin's
stag do. Heard he died on the spot'.

Just like that, in the blink of an eye her Ken was gone. The
colour had drained from her face and she felt unsteady on
her feet.

'You alright love, you look ever so pale? The women
looked concerned.

Edna felt her legs go beneath her and before she could stop
herself she fainted. When she came round, she could hear
Mr Smith who owned the shop. 'You alright love? you gave
us such a fright? A few people had gathered around her and
someone had stuck some smelling salts under her nose.

Edna could not speak; the words would not come out. Her
Ken had been stabbed and was dead. He was not coming
back. Edna felt the first prick of tears start to form in the
corner of her eyes. She had to get out of here; she had to
say something.

'I'm fine, so sorry, I didn't eat any breakfast this morning,
silly me.'

She started to get to her feet but still felt light headed. She
just had to get out of this shop. The shop where her Ken

used to work, where he used to greet her with a wink and a smile, who serenaded her and made her feel like a movie star. She managed to get to her feet, smoothed her clothes down, thanked everyone for being so kind before she turned and left the shop. She did not know where she was going at first but she had ended up at the Arboretum she and Ken used to visit and headed straight to the bench they used to share. Edna slumped onto the bench and cried her heart out.

She later learned that during his cousin's stag night, a fight had broken out and Ken had been stabbed. His cousin had got into an argument with someone in the pub and Ken being the kind, gentle peacemaker, tried to intervene and break it up. One of the man's friends was the one to stab Ken who had tragically died on the way to the hospital.

Her heart was broken and things were never the same for Edna. After Ken's death, Edna concentrated on nursing her mother until her death. She never told her about Ken, after all it was too late now.

As Edna left school early, she did not have the relevant qualifications or the skills to do office work. She was able to read and write and she had been adept at maths and it was these skills that led her to work at Uptown Cinema.

Edna came back to the present and looked at the wall clock; it was showing 7:00am. Edna rose wearily from the chair to get ready for work. She was on the early shift today. Before leaving her house she made sure her 'babies' were fed and watered having enough food for the day before leaving to go to work. Edna arrived at work at 9:30am. She moved quickly through the foyer and towards the steps, making her way downstairs before anyone could see her.

Today had not been a great day, the projectors were not working. When Edna got down to the freezer room she found that the electrics had blown through the night causing all the freezers to go off. All of the ice creams and ice lollies had melted. It looked like a total mess. Edna did not panic or lose her head as Sylvia was doing at this very moment. Edna took a deep breath then went about the business of cleaning up all the mess. Edna loved working in the freezer room. This was her own private Idaho and she loved every minute of it. Edna was not one for the hustle and bustle of the comings and goings of customers and having to deal with their complaints and gripes. Down here it was peaceful and quiet and she was in total control. She ensured that all the fridges were always full with choc ices, ice creams and ice lollies and that they were always in tip top condition.

The freezer room stocked three large chest freezers and Edna had a chair at the back of these. There was a small table beside her chair with a small radio on it. As long as she had her radio tuned to Radio 4 she was a happy bunny. No one really bothered her down here and she did not bother them. During interval time, there would be a flurry of girls coming in and out filling up their trays to serve to the customers and they would have the occasional conversation with her.

All of the girls who worked there were young compared to Edna so they found it difficult to strike up a conversation with her. Only Reama had made more of an effort to speak with her and she had developed a fondness for her. She had worked with Brenda and Sylvia for over 20 years and still did not know who they really were. She had not had much of a conversation with them throughout that time. In the early days they had made an effort with her and used to invite her out with them but she always made up some excuse or another not to go.

In the end they had given up asking her and left her to her own devices. In truth Edna was a loner and had been that way for most of her life. She was never a great conversationalist and never really had any friends whilst growing up. Apart from her beloved Radio 4, Edna had also developed a keen interest in tennis. Every year she would take two weeks off work to watch Wimbledon. This is where she belonged now and where she felt some peace.

Chapter 7: Sue and Tracey

Sue was only nine years old when she and her family moved to the same area as Tracey. Her family had been like nomads, moving around mainly in the North of the country for most of her life. Not really stopping in one place long enough for her to get to make any real friends. Sue was the youngest of five children who were a few years older than her. Her parents had been married to other people before they met and had Sue when they were in their late forties. She got on well with her siblings who had remained living in their local area, but she felt like an only child growing up. The only thing she had was her beloved dog called Sheba whom she had since she was a puppy. She was a border collie with a beautiful thick, black shiny coat of fur who had a distinct head shape that looked like a triangle when you faced her straight on.

Sue remembered living for a time in the countryside in a beautiful five bedroomed farmhouse. There were horses in a nearby field, whose owner had said she could help to look after them. She also learned how to ride and had a favourite horse in particular whom she called Polo. This was one of her most favourite places to live and she had missed everything about living there. Her parents were carers of adults with learning disabilities who lived within their home. They had been doing this for as long as Sue could remember. She had come to know and care for many herself. Most of the adults had only stayed for a short time but there were two who had been with them for as long as she could remember. They were called Malcolm and Audrey who were both in their early twenties, but acted a lot younger than that.

When her parents had announced that they were moving again, Sue was awash with the usual feelings of anxiety and dread. This would've meant having to move to a new school and getting to know new people all over again. The good thing was Malcom and Audrey would be coming with them as well as Sheba. It had been the start of the summer holidays so she would have six weeks to try and make friends before she started school.

The house they had moved into was huge. It had six bedrooms and sat in a large corner plot at the top of the street. There had been a large garden at the front which was accessed at the top of the street through a wooden gate with an even bigger garden at the back. She had chosen one of the rooms in the attic as it overlooked the whole street. She could see into the local park which was a few streets away. Her bedroom was large enough to have a double bed, a white double toy boy wardrobe and a large Chest of six drawers to match. Her dad had asked her what colour she wanted for her room and she had chosen white and pink walls with a deep blue carpet. She then filled her walls with pictures of the latest pop stars she was in love with.

They had been living in the house for a couple of weeks when her mum asked her to run to the local shop to get some milk and bread. It had been a warm sunny day, so Sue had put on red denim shorts and a white short sleeved blouse. She put on some white plimsolls and put her hair up in a bun. She had walked to the shop which was across the road from the park. The one she could see from her bedroom window. She had glimpsed someone playing on the swings and for a moment thought it was a boy. She went into the shop and got the things her mum asked for and on the way back home Sue met Tracey for the first time.

Tracey had been in the park for a while and was playing on the swings by herself.   She was feeling lonely. She wondered if she would ever have any friends, why no one liked her and her family and never wanted to play with them. Tracey knew her family was not perfect. She had come from a large family of nine children and she had been the sixth child. She had two younger brothers and a sister with three older brothers and two sisters. Her oldest brother Timmy had been sent to prison for breaking and entering people's houses. This did not go down well with their neighbours. The two other older ones were not much better and had been linked to a series of burglaries and car thefts. It was only a matter of time before they would be sent to a young offender's institute. Her family were notoriously known in the local area for their criminal activities with her father being at the head of this. Her father had spent most of her life in and out of prison and had encouraged his sons to follow in his footsteps. Her two younger brothers were catching up fast behind their older brothers and were already known to the police as well as the local shopkeepers and neighbours.

The family lived in a semi-detached three bedroom council house. It was not big enough for the family to live in, but she knew the council would not move them as her parents had been in a lot of rent arrears. Their parents had the grace to give them the rooms upstairs and made the living room into their own bedroom. The youngest three children had a room. Tracey shared with her two older sisters and the oldest boys had occupied the third room, which had a bunk bed and a single mattress on the floor. The room she shared with her sisters was big enough for a double bed which they all slept on. The walls had peeling wallpaper and there was evidence of dampness in one corner. The window, which overlooked the overgrown back garden, had a hairline crack going from corner to corner. It would be a matter of time before it would break. There had been one second hand double wardrobe in their room and clothes were piled high in one corner; as they had no room to hang anything. The carpet was old and fraying at the edges and the room smelled of damp and stale sweat.

Tracey got on ok with her sisters and her eldest sister Amanda, who at thirteen years old was the one responsible for looking after the youngest children when her parents were too drunk to even notice they existed. Tracey knew her family was different from other families. Their home was messy, dirty and cluttered with clothes and rubbish everywhere. Her parents had neglected their children's personal and physical care and did not care much about housework. Tracey had often worn dirty clothes because their mum could not be bothered to wash them. Amanda tried her best, but there had been a lot of kids to look after. It was a regular thing for them to get up and get dressed without having a wash or something to eat and would often turn up at school looking tired, hungry and dishevelled. The other children would distance themselves from them and often call them tramps or smelly.

Tracey felt ashamed of herself and her family even at her young age. She promised herself, once again, that when she was older; things would be different for her. She would wear new clean clothes that smelled of fabric conditioner. She would always have a wash, look good and smell clean and tidy.

Tracey had spotted the new girl earlier on before she entered the shop. She had not seen her before and she became curious as to who she was and where she came from. As the girl emerged from the shop, Tracey did not know why, but she had jumped off the swings, ran out of the park and started to walk behind her. She had liked what this girl was wearing and wished that she could wear something like that. She briefly looked down at her worn out trainers, grubby green shorts and a stained blue T shirt before continuing behind her.

Out of the corner of her eye, Sue had seen Tracey come off the swings and run out of the park and knew instinctively she was following behind her. Sue deliberately slowed down her pace, in the hope she would catch up with her. Sue had walked a few yards before she heard her say; "Are you new around here"? Sue stopped, turned round and saw Tracey for the first time. She noticed she had been about the same height as her and really skinny. She had short mousey brown hair that looked like someone had cut around it with a bowl and a pair of blunt scissors. It was so short it made her look like a boy at first glance. She had the biggest round brown eyes she had ever seen which sat under the thickest bushiest eyebrows ever. She was wearing green shorts and a blue T shirt that did not look very clean, but the other thing Sue remembered was the smell. When she had stood in front of Tracey she had caught the overpowering smell of urine and when she had moved closer towards her she noticed that her face looked dirty as did her hands and nails. Despite this, it did not put Sue off at all. In fact it had endeared her to Tracey even more and she could not understand why; not then anyway. "Yes I am. I moved around the corner from here with my parents. Our house is the one on the corner at the top of the street".

"You must be the rich girl everyone is talking about. The rich family in the big corner house. What's your name?."

"Sue. What's yours?"

"Tracey. How old are you?"

"Nine"

"Me too. Do you wanna be my friend?"

"Ok"

And that was it. In that moment Sue and Tracey forged a friendship that was to last for many years as they became inseparable. They had spent the rest of the summer together and were pleased they were to be in the same school. They were lucky to get to be in the same class together throughout the whole of junior and senior school. Even when other children tried to get in between her friendship with Tracey, Sue would not allow this and had been fiercely protective of her. They had formed a strong bond and connection and Sue had developed a loyalty towards Tracey so fierce she believed that only death could have separated them.

When Sue turned sixteen, her parents decided to move up north again. This did not come as a surprise to Sue who was more taken aback, that they had not moved sooner. Her parents, especially her mum, had been itching to move for a while now but had decided to stay until Sue had finished school. It came as no surprise to her parents either that Sue did not want to go with them or that Tracey would be moving in with her.

This was the longest time Sue had lived in one place. It was the first time she had found stability and friends and she was not ready to give this up. Apart from Tracey, Sue had made many friends in the area and had become quite a popular person. She had developed the type of character and personality people warmed to immediately and she was a nice person who was easy to get along with.

Sue's parents had bought a few properties some years earlier which housed adults with learning disabilities who were more able to live independently but with support. One of the nearby houses had a large room which had been unoccupied for a few months. Sue had suggested she move in there to which her parents happily agreed.

After they left school, they started at the same college and enrolled on the same course; a secretarial programme. When they turned seventeen, for extra cash, Sue and Tracey went to work at Uptown Cinema. Sue had got the job of working the Kiosk and the bar in the evenings and Tracey worked as an usherette. They loved working at Uptown Cinema and had made many friends there. After working there for six months, Sue and Tracey both decided to drop out of college and work at Uptown Cinema full time.

Sue and Tracey worked hard and played even harder; going out every weekend after work and sometimes during the week too. There had been many occasions when they had turned up at work late the following day, still intoxicated by the amount of alcohol they had consumed the night before.

Within the year, Sue and Tracey decided to get a bigger flat together. They moved from the room Tracey had shared with Sue into a two bedroom flat just on the outskirts of the inner city. They had seen the flat advertised in the local paper and on their rare days off together both went to see it. They loved the place as soon as they saw it. The flat was on the second floor and had been one of sixteen flats. There was a lift as well as stairs and access was by an intercom. The flat was quite large and spacious with two good sized bedrooms with Magnolia painted walls and grey carpet, separated by a bathroom. At the top of the long corridor was a separate toilet and at the end was a large living area with a good sized kitchen. It was perfect. They had paid their deposit as soon as they could and had moved in a few weeks later.

Sue knew she had been lucky and had had a charmed life. Despite all the moving around in her early life, Sue had a brilliant and loving relationship with her parents who always loved and cared for her. Sue had never gone without anything and knew she had been spoiled rotten by her parents who doted on her. She spoke to her parents almost every day on the phone and would visit them as often as she could. Sue's parents had thought her relationship with Tracey was great and had been proud of how she had become friends with her. They found Tracey a little strange at first and had felt sorry for her because of the way she had been brought up. They never passed comments nor did they judge Tracey or her family despite knowing the family's reputation. In fact, in some ways, Sue felt her parents had encouraged their relationship. They always encouraged her to invite Tracey over for tea and dinner and suggested she come along with them on family holidays and day trips to the seaside. Tracey had even spent a week with them in Wales and they had an amazing time staying in a large caravan. Tracey was always staying over at Sue's house and as she got older she stayed more often slowly distancing herself from her family. Sue could never understand Tracey's family or why her parents did not look after them the way her parents looked after her. Tracey used to say she was adopted and that when she got older, she would find her parents who would still be together, had been looking for her and would be very rich!! They would then welcome her back by showering her with gifts, money and lots of clothes!

Chapter 8: The secrets we keep

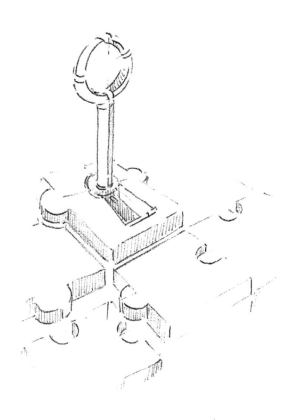

Sue loved working in the Kiosk. During the day she would sell an endless flow of popcorn, hot dogs, chocolate, sweets and fizzy drinks. She loved smiling, chatting and interacting with customers and had even been on a date or two with some of them. She mainly worked with Brenda, an older woman who had been working at Uptown Cinema for years. She liked Brenda and they got on and worked well together. Sue had heard the rumours about Brenda and the doorman Bill but kept this to herself. She also knew Brenda was married with two grown up children but Brenda looked happy and commented to her that she had never felt happier and alive in her life.

Sue wondered if she would ever be in an amazing relationship and have the perfect love. She had been in plenty of relationships and constantly met guys on nights out with Tracey but these relationships had not lasted or had quickly fizzled out leaving Sue unfulfilled and empty inside. Deep down in her heart Sue knew what she wanted, what would make her happier than she had ever been but quickly turned these thoughts off. It was not good for Sue to think like that. Sue had often thought she was a lesbian growing up. Back then being gay was not something she could even consider. She remembered there had been two women living together where she was growing up and when the local kids got wind of this they made their lives hell; throwing stones at them, smashing their windows and name calling. In the end things got so bad they had moved away.

So Sue had ignored her feelings towards women and hoped they would go away. Unsurprisingly, they did not. It took Sue a while to pluck up the courage to tell her parents she was gay. In truth Sue absolutely could not raise the subject with them. Not because she was scared of them being homophobic, but because she just was not used to speaking to them in that way. In the end, instead of a face to face conversation, she wrote it all down in a letter because she wanted to be able to say everything she needed to.

It took them less than a week to get in touch following that letter - but it seemed like a lifetime to Sue. They asked her to come and visit and sat her down and said that they knew and that they loved her. They had said she was their daughter and just wanted her to be happy. Her mum had hoped coming out would make her happy. Sue had said she hoped so too but had asked them not to say anything. That had been two years ago and they were yet to see how fulfilled and happy her life could be. Her parents had completely accepted Sue for who she was and had asked if she was in love with Tracey; they had suspected this for a long while. Sue had been taken aback by her parent's brutal honesty and had broken down crying admitting how she had felt about her, but that Tracey did not know how she felt or that she was gay.

Somewhere along the way, Sue had told her siblings, but to be honest the only people who she really cared about knowing were her parents. Despite not really growing up with her older siblings, who had lives of their own. Sue knew her family would do anything for each other but as siblings, they never really had big heart to heart conversations. When she eventually told them, it was not out of her own willingness, but because she found out that her dad had been talking to her brother about it. She knew that if he knew, it would not be long before the others did too. She knew she had to tell them all to avoid being uncomfortable in family situations. It was over quite quick and the conversation just went on to something else. They said they had always had an inkling and that they just wanted Sue to be happy. She had left feeling quite liberated and had asked herself why she did not tell them all those years ago. Sue had not yet told anyone at work. Everyone at work thought she was a single, straight girl. She knew she should tell them and she wanted to, but she needed to know how Tracey felt about her first.

Sue remembered the day she had fallen in love with Tracey and wondered if her feelings went way further back than that. They had been sixteen and pretty much living together by then. They had gone out one night and had gotten absolutely blind drunk. At sixteen, both had looked much older than their years making it easy to get served in the bars and pubs they frequented. No one ever questioned their age nor were they suspicious of this. They had staggered out of a late night bar laughing and joking and had bought some chips and a kebab from a local chip shop before jumping into a taxi to get home. When they got home they were eating their food and talking about the night's events. Tracey had been chatted up by a guy who had obviously overused tanning lotion and who had the whitest teeth she had ever seen. The bar had been packed full of people smoking and drinking and the air conditioning seemed to have been turned off (bars normally do this to encourage the customers to buy more drinks). As the guy continued to drone on about his work in an office and how he liked to work out at the gym, Tracey noticed that his face started to streak due to the heat and sweat. As the beads of sweat started to appear on his forehead and slowly dripped down, it merged with the poorly applied tanning lotion which peeled it off in lines. Tracey tried her best not to laugh and, in the end, excused herself to go to the toilet before falling into fits of laughter with Sue.

Tracey loved going out with Sue and enjoyed her company. She loved her like a sister; probably loved her more than she did her own sisters. Tracey became serious and still intoxicated by the night's consumption of alcohol, she told Sue how thankful she was that they were friends. How grateful she was to Sue's family, who had welcomed her with open arms, never judged her for who her family were and how she never had any friends before she came along. She turned to Sue and gave her a big hug.

"I really love you Sue"

"I love you too Tracey".

Sue did not know what she was thinking or what came over her but she leaned in towards Tracey and kissed her on the lips. Tracey jolted back, pushed Sue away from her and jumped to her feet immediately sobering up.

"What the fuck, d'you think you're doing?"

"I err, I don't' know, I just thought"

"Thought, what exactly?"

"You, you said you loved me"

"As a fucking sister, I love you like a sister Sue, that's all!"

"I'm, I'm so sorry Tracey, really I am. I wasn't thinking"

"You fucking better be sorry Sue, I ain't no lesbian and neither are you!"

"I'm drunk and got a bit carried away. I am really sorry Tracey your right I ain't no lesbian"

"Damn right you're not, you just got fucking carried away"

"I promise Tracey, it won't happen again, I swear"

In that moment Sue realised two things; one she was in love with Tracey and two she could never admit that to her. She was devastated.

The next morning, Sue woke up with a blinding headache and was feeling exhausted. After last night she and Tracey had each gone to their own beds without saying another word to each other. It was especially awkward as they were still sharing just one room. Sue crept out of her bed so as not to wake Tracey, quickly showered and dressed herself and left for work. That day had been Tracey's day off and Sue's shift did not start until 11:00am but she had left the house early so she did not have to see or speak with Tracey. Sue was still reeling from the previous night's events and was still figuring out what had come over her and compelled her to kiss Tracey like that.

When she had got into work, Elaine, Reama and Anton were all in the staff room getting ready to start their shifts. Sue had contemplated telling Reama what happened last night but quickly dismissed this. The less people knew about this the better, she was not ready to come out of the closet just yet. As she was thinking about what happened the night before, out of the corner of her eye, she saw Elaine dart quickly towards the staff toilet. This had reminded Sue of how recently she had noticed that Elaine had been looking really thin and had lost some weight. She also knew that Elaine was a gym fanatic and was always working out and on some diet plan or another and had put it down to this. However, she had an uneasy feeling that things were not what they seemed with Elaine; she just could not put her finger on it.

Tracey had lain in bed long after Sue had left the house. She was still running through the events of the previous night and trying to make sense of it. She kept asking herself what she had done or said to Sue to make her think that it was ok to kiss her. She was no lesbian that was for sure, but she did not even imagine that Sue was either. All the time she had known Sue, she had never had any reason to suspect that Sue was gay. She had been her best friend since she was nine years old, how could she not know this. Every time they went on a night out, Sue would always pull a guy, sometimes more so than Tracey. Sue did not look like a lesbian or dress like one either. She had worn her hair short in a Pageboy style but a lot of girls were wearing their hair like that at the moment, it was fashionable. It just did not make sense to Tracey. If Sue was gay, why did she not tell her? She was sure she would.

Tracey had been telling the truth when she had told Sue she loved her but only as a sister. Even though Tracey had three sisters of her own, she was never really that close to them. In fact she was never really that close to her family at all. Tracey had been ashamed of her family and the way they had lived and she had really resented this. Tracey never felt that her parents had loved her or her siblings and she had never felt that she had loved them. She had just been existing, waiting for the time when she could leave them all behind. Conditions at home had not changed much over the years and when Sue asked her to live with her, she jumped at the chance. Sue's parents had decided to move back up North and Sue did not want to go with them. They had owned a house with a large spare room and Sue had asked them if she could have it. Sue had turned up at her house so excited and could not wait to tell her. "Guess what? My parents said I can have a room in a house that they own!!"

"Really?"

"Yes, and it's big enough for the two of us!!"

Tracey could not believe her ears. She didn't care that they had to share a room together, after all she had been sharing with her sisters for most of her life and Sue was like a sister to her albeit a better one. When she had told her parents she was leaving, they did not bat an eyelid. Her mother had muttered something about Tracey thinking she was better than them and to be honest she was not wrong. Tracey wanted a better life for herself; she wanted to live in a clean home with clean clothes and nothing was going to stop her from getting this. Tracey remembered even as a young child trying to clean and tidy up her bedroom. It had been difficult sharing a room with two other people who were as messy and disgusting as their parents. Within hours of cleaning her room, it would revert back to a messy chaotic state. None of her sisters had cared how the room looked, but Tracey did. Her siblings were certainly her parent's children and took after them. Tracey was so grateful for the opportunity she could not leave her house fast enough.

Luckily, the room was big enough to fit in two single beds, single wardrobes and a large chest of drawers they shared. Sharing a room with Sue had not been too bad as she was quite tidy, although Tracey felt she could make more of an effort. Tracey had developed an obsession with cleaning and was always washing and tidying up. Even if it was Sue's turn to do the washing up Tracey would still re-wash and re-clean the sink, sides and cupboard doors. Everything had a perfect place of their own in their kitchen. Sue often teased her about this, but Tracey did not care as long as everything was clean, tidy and dust free. Sue could say what she wanted. On Tracey's side of the room, everything had its place. Her clothes were hung in the wardrobe; co-ordinated by what items they were such as skirts, dresses, trousers and jeans. Each had their own perfect place. At the bottom of the wardrobe were her carefully placed colour co-ordinated shoes in a range of different styles.

Tracey also loved shopping and wearing the latest affordable fashionable clothes. She liked to look good and well turned out and would spend hours looking through magazines for the latest fashionable clothes before buying the high street versions of this. She told herself that one day she would be in a position to afford the real designer labels. Every night before going to bed, Tracey would take a bath or a shower and every morning she made sure she showered for at least twenty minutes. Her common sense told her she was behaving in an over the top way. She figured this was as a result of how she was brought up and the stench she was sure she could still faintly smell was what she wanted to get rid of.

Tracey rarely talked about her family and could not remember the last time she had visited her parents or seen her siblings. She knew that they still lived in the same house she grew up in and that things hadn't changed much. She knew that both her older two brothers and her dad were doing ten years for attempted armed robbery. She had read it in the local papers and could feel herself getting washed over with shame at just thinking about them. She wondered again for the hundredth time how some parents were allowed to get away with having children and not look after them properly or give them the love and affection they deserved? Where had the Social Services been? Tracey felt she would have been a lot better off in care. Her parents were despicable human beings and the further she stayed away from them the better. A few years back she used to see some of her siblings around. If they ever came to the cinema to watch a movie, she would make up every excuse to not have to see or speak with them. Amanda got married at seventeen, moved to the other side of town and had two children of her own. Michelle had one child and was living quite close to her parents; something she could not understand. Patrick, her younger brother and two sisters still lived at home and very rarely had contact with her.

Tracey had seen her brother Patrick out in town once. She and Sue had been in a busy bar deep in conversation. Out of the blue he had come up to her and had been abusive, saying she thought she was better than the rest of the family and was too nice to even visit them. He said that their parents did not want anything to do with a snotty nosed bitch like her and that she could rot in hell!! Tracey never said a word in response to his tirade of abuse and had turned around and walked off. She had not been hurt by his words, more offended that her parents did not want anything to do with her. The cheek of it. They had not cared then and they did not care now so to hell with the lot of them!! That was a few years ago and Tracey had moved on since then. Sue and Tracey had managed to rent a bigger flat and they each had their own room and their own space. Neither Tracey nor Sue raised the subject of that night again and they continued to party as if it never happened. They both continued to drift in and out of meaningless relationships and one-night stands, but each had their own secret desires and unmet needs.

When Tracey first met Anton, she was immediately attracted to and smitten by him. It was his eyes that attracted her to him and the way he looked at her; like he could really see her and she knew that she wanted him there and then. Tracey knew he had a girlfriend but this did not put her off. She had even met Isabelle once on a night out, who seemed a nice person but she had wanted Anton in a way that made her body physically ache whenever he was near her. Besides, Isabelle was Anton's problem not hers.

Her relationship with Anton started after a staff night out. As most of them were similar in age, they often went out after work. There had been Sue, Reama, Elaine and a couple of newbies who had started a few weeks earlier. They had done the usual pub crawl around town before ending up at a trendy new late night bar which opened up a few months earlier. They had settled themselves in a corner and the drinks and chatter started to flow freely. Tracey had managed to manoeuvre herself next to Anton so he would notice her. Tracey always liked to look good but tonight she had made an extra effort. She had worn a short, tight panelled blue and white dress. It had thin straps which fell into a sweetheart shape which showed off the top of her breasts. When she sat down the dress rode up revealing her thighs. Tracey knew she looked amazing and she hoped Anton would too.

As the night went on the others started to say their goodbyes and head off home and in the end, it was just Sue, Tracey and Anton left. Sue had been talking to a guy at the other end of the bar which left just Anton and Tracey together. As usual Tracey had had too much to drink but not enough to pluck up the courage to make the move she had been anticipating for a while on Anton. She had been flirting with him all night and he had flirted back so she leaned in and kissed him on his lips. Tracey was delighted that he had reacted and kissed her back.

Sue had decided to go back to the guy's place she had met earlier which pleased Tracey even more who seized the opportunity to invite Anton back to her flat. She had been elated when Anton agreed to go back with her. As soon as they got back to her flat, they wasted no time in going to her room and getting undressed. The sex had been exactly how she imagined it would be and much more. Anton was a considerate lover who had touched and caressed her in ways she had never experienced before, her body setting alight and feeling like a raging fire. Anton had been insatiable and Tracey could not get enough of him. One thing was for sure, if she was to have it her way, this was not going to be a one-night stand.

Early the following morning, Anton had acted a little cool and aloof and Tracey had been a little upset by this but did not show it. Despite his aloofness, they had sex again which was just as pleasurable as the night before and Tracey just drank him in. She knew she was falling for him in a big way but she did not care, as she needed him more than she had ever needed anyone in her life. It did not matter that they hardly spoke afterwards or that after Anton had gone into the bathroom to shower he had asked her not to tell anyone about what had happened between them. Tracey had agreed but only on the basis they carried on seeing each other. At that moment, Tracey realised that despite how she felt about Anton, the feeling was not mutual but this little detail did not deter her. As long as he carried on seeing her that would be enough for her, at least for now.

Chapter 9: Bill and Brenda

Brenda slipped out of the stock room, being careful no one saw her and a few seconds later Bill had followed. Brenda made her way to the toilets to freshen up. She looked in the mirror and wondered how much longer this was going to go on for and that she was gettin.g far too old to be having sneaky sex whenever the fancy took her. To tell the truth she did not care.

For the first time in years Brenda had felt alive, she had not known such pleasure and excitement in such a long time, if ever and she was revelling in it. It was not that she didn't love her husband or would ever leave him, she was happy with Ted but their sex life had died a sudden death a few years previously. Brenda also no longer had any desire for Ted like she used to and their relationship had turned into mainly that of friendship, comfortability and companionship.

They no longer slept in the same bedroom anymore. Ted's snoring had gotten so bad over the years that the only way she could get a decent night's sleep was for her to go into another room. This continued over the years. In the end, Brenda had grown to enjoy this peace and solitude so it remained that way ever since. Ted had just got used to the idea and never said anything about it.

Brenda and Ted had been married for nearly thirty five years and had two children, a girl and a boy. Her children were all grown up now and no longer needed her as much as they did before. They were old enough to live their own lives and had left home a while ago, so Brenda no longer had that role of mother to two small children. At fifty five Brenda felt she still looked good for her age. The years had been kind to her and she had aged well, unlike some of her friends who looked haggard and tired all the time.

Brenda's deep set blue eyes still burned with fire and looked young and alive as it did when she was in her teens. Despite the knowing signs of the dreaded crow's feet developing underneath them, if she could afford cosmetic surgery she knew she would. She would have the whole lot done; eyes, cheeks, neck, nose, lifts and tucks. She kept the increasingly growing grey hairs at bay with a good bottle of bleach blonde hair dye; a similar colour to that in her youth.

Brenda had known Ted all of her life; they had been neighbours as children so had grown up together. From as far back as she could remember, Brenda knew she would end up marrying Ted. They had started dating when she was fourteen and when Ted eventually proposed to her at eighteen, she did not hesitate to say yes. They had gone on to have a large wedding when she turned twenty with over four hundred guests.

Each of them had come from large families with extended families who all lived nearby. Brenda herself was one of nine children, whilst Ted was one of seven. In the end both of their families had contributed towards the cost of the reception and had to extend the local community centre to accommodate everyone. It had been one of the happiest days of Brenda's life. Brenda had settled quickly into married life and eventually into motherhood. She had suffered three miscarriages at the beginning but then she eventually gave birth to a healthy girl followed by a healthy boy eighteen months later.

Brenda had adored her family and loved her children and husband with everything she had. She loved staying at home and being the best wife and mother she could be. The children were always immaculately dressed, she kept a beautiful home and always made sure meals were ready for when Ted came home from work. She even made sure that she fulfilled her wifely duties within the bedroom and they had had a good sex life.

As the years went by and the children started school, Brenda had started to become bored and restless. In the end it had been Ted who suggested she take a part time job. Brenda had done ok at school but knew she did not have the qualifications to do an office job and she certainly wanted to avoid working in the local knicker factory. She had looked through the papers and had seen the advert for a cashier at Uptown Cinema. She always liked the idea of working in a movie theatre so had applied for this and been successful.

Brenda had enjoyed working in the little booth at the front of the building, taking the stream of customers' money who came to visit on a regular basis. As time went by, she had moved up to work as a cashier in the Kiosk which included working the bar and she absolutely loved this job. When the children had left school, Brenda decided to work full time and she welcomed the independence and freedom this gave her.

Over the years Brenda and Ted had fallen into a mundane routine. Ted would go to the pub with his friends twice a week. Every year they would hire a caravan and spend a week at the same seaside coast. Brenda had loved going to the coast with Ted especially when the children were younger. She had cherished those family moments. As the children got older and got on with their own lives, things were not the same. Brenda was starting to tire of this life and the same routines. She had started to crave for something more and exciting.

Chapter 10: About Bill

Bill was a man in his late fifties who had come to work at Uptown Cinema as a Doorman. He had been divorced for nearly fifteen years. He had been in a few relationships with all kinds of women, but he had not met anyone enough to want to settle down with.

Bill had put this down to his own childhood and how his mum had abandoned him as a young child. He had been the youngest of two children, having an older sister called Dotty who was five years older than him. He had no contact with her and he last saw when he was twenty five years old at their father's funeral. His sister Dotty's childhood had also been cut short the day their mum left, as she had no choice but to take on the role of a mother and care for Bill. She had been resentful of this role as far back as he could remember and the bitterness only deepened as they got older.

As soon as he had reached fourteen, his sister had upped and left after marrying the first man she dated and he had not seen her since; not even getting an invite to her wedding. Dotty never had any children of her own and he suspected that this had to do with the fact that she had to leave school and look after him.

Bill remembered coming home from school one day and when he arrived home, he immediately knew something was wrong. There was not the usual smell of food cooking in the kitchen and the radio was not playing one of his mum's favourite tunes. He felt a sense of dread as he tiptoed slowly into the house. He had seen his father at the kitchen table with his head in his hands and there was an almost empty bottle of whisky in front of him.

Bill had heard whimpering coming from his dad and the dread he felt earlier grew bigger and bigger as fear started to grip him. His hand had started to hurt and when he looked down, he had been gripping the bannister so tight his knuckles had turned white. Bill had no clue what to do and had stood transfixed at the bottom of the stairs for what seemed like an eternity. He was unable to move and his eyes remained transfixed at the lowly figure he saw in front of him. At first Bill did not hear what his sister had said and for a moment he thought it was his mum's voice until it grew louder in his ear.

'Get upstairs, now, I need to talk to you'

She had practically dragged him up the stairs to his room before quickly closing the door.

'Where's mum?', the words came out as a small whisper, too frightened to say it any louder in case his dad had heard.

'She's gone Bill'

'Gone where?, is she coming back?'

'No'. At that Dotty had sat on his bed and started to cry.

Bill stood staring at his sister trying to take in what she had said to him. He walked over to his sister who held him in her arms, and he started to cry. Things were different from then. His dad had become more distant from him as he drank more and more each day. Friends and the family he remembered had rallied round at first, but his dad's drinking and destructive behaviour had eventually driven them away. Bill had relied on his sister for everything as his dad, in his own devastation, had ignored him. Bill had developed a fear of being left abandoned since then. He would constantly have this fear that his sister would leave even though she was becoming more and more disgruntled about having to care for him.

By the time he reached thirteen, his dad had all but checked out of his life. His drinking had eventually consumed him, and he was left an empty shell and out of reach for any emotional affection he needed. The relationship between him and his sister had become strained and she had been spending less and less time at home which meant he had to fend for himself. He had learned very quickly he would have to rely on himself and resolved to take care of himself.

Up to this day, Bill never knew the real reason why his mum left. He had heard people whispering whenever he was in the local shop or post office not long after she left; that she had run off with another man.

Over the years, Bill had formed an inability to form healthy relationships with anyone. He had become a bit of a loner, preferring it that way. At times he had 'checked out of relationships or even friendships, feeling unattached or emotionally unavailable to connect to anyone. Bill had gone through a period where he had developed poor self-esteem and feelings of low self-worth. He suffered from anxiety and depression often feeling that he was not good enough, so he had steered clear of relationships.

He had come close once with a woman called Audrey Jackson. She had been beautiful with long black hair, brown eyes and a body to die for. Audrey had been a few years younger than him, they had been together for about five years and had shared some good times together. She had been easy to talk to and had a great sense of humour, was kind and generous too, but Audrey Jackson also had a side to her that he did not like. Audrey had a violent temper which was made worse when she was drunk, and if cursing had been an Olympic sport she would have won the gold medal every time. It was that which had driven him away in the end. She had never physically been violent towards him by attacking him with her fists, but she would pick up things and throw them at him. During their stormy relationship Bill had been the target of plates, cups, cutlery, furniture, household goods, anything Audrey could get her hands on when she was drunk. It was not a pleasant sight, but she had been so self-destructive after experiencing a traumatic event in her childhood and he had both loved and felt sorry for her at the same time. He knew he held onto this relationship, even if it was unhealthy, to avoid any feelings of abandonment or loneliness. In the end it had become too much and he had told her that he could not stay with her and that she needed help. That had been over two years ago and during that time he had learned to be happy living on his own and enjoying his own company.

Bill had been working as a labourer over the years and was getting sick of the early hours, long days, not always the guarantee of work and low wages. He had been working on a building site and had been moaning about the work and wanting to do something different when one of the lads had mentioned that his cousin was working at the cinema and they were looking for Doormen. As Bill wanted to do something different, he applied for the job at Uptown Cinema, had been successful and started work the following week.

Bill had noticed Brenda almost straight away but knew instinctively that she was also married; he could tell the type straight away before even seeing the ring. Bill had always made a pledge not to get involved with married women as they always seemed to bring nothing but trouble; at least that is what his friends had said. Nevertheless Bill had felt an immediate attraction towards Brenda and was taken aback by her startling blue eyes and the air of confidence she had which bounced off her in rays. He was definitely smitten alright.

Bill loved working at Uptown Cinema and enjoyed being a Doorman. His job was to ensure the safety of the public, exiting difficult customers, chasing young teenagers who had sneaked in through the exit doors, general customer service, spot cleaning the front area, and undertaking some minor maintenance. He loved his Uniform which was blue with matching blue trousers and jacket with a yellow shirt and brown tie and ensured he always maintained a clean-cut appearance and cheerful attitude. Bill knew it was not a highly skilled job, but he took every pride in this.

About six months into his job, Bill had been asked to help move the Popcorn machine around in the Kiosk and Brenda had been on shift. The Kiosk was not very big nor was it wide enough for two people to pass comfortably by. Bill needed to get to the other side of the Kiosk where Brenda was standing and had to move past her to get there. As he went to move past Brenda, he felt a strong physical pull and for an instant they locked eyes on each other before Brenda quickly averted her gaze. For a moment he felt that the wind had been knocked out of him and he was unable to breathe. Bill composed himself very quickly but had been left a little shaken by this.

Brenda became quiet and shy and had felt her face flush. This was most unlike her and she struggled to know what to do so she started giving Bill orders about what he needed to do with the popcorn machine, where it should go, it was heavy, did he need help with it; on and on. She had been taken aback by that moment and Bill could tell she had felt it too.

Brenda was surprised by what had come over her. She had

spoken to Bill from time to time since he began working at Uptown Cinema and there had been times when they had shared the odd joke or two. Brenda was aware of how handsome Bill was and she had liked his cheeky chappie persona. Sometimes when they were talking, he would wink at her but she had just put this down to harmless flirting but today had been different.

When Bill had gone to move past her, Brenda had been all too aware of the physical pull she had felt and how embarrassed and flustered she had become. She also knew that he had felt the same way but she was way too embarrassed to say anything. Besides, she was a married woman. Brenda had started to make idle chatter in a desperate bid that how she was feeling would go away but it did not. In the end she had made up some excuse before leaving the Kiosk as quickly as she could. After that incident, Brenda had made a conscious effort to avoid Bill until the night of the work Christmas party.

Chapter 11: The Christmas Party

Uptown Cinema's General Manager had always arranged for the annual Christmas party to take place on work premises. Apart from Christmas and New Year's Eve, this was the only other time Uptown Cinema doors would be closed early and he would arrange for caterers to come in and provide the most extravagant Christmas buffet fit for royalty.

There were prawn vol-au-vents, pigs in blankets, cheese and pineapple sticks, mini pork pies, cheese straws, Yorkshire puddings with sliced beef and horseradish, smoked salmon and cream cheese, sausage rolls, mince pies etc. There was a vast amount of alcohol flowing, music courtesy of a local DJ and lots and lots of laughter.

Over the years, it had been Ted who would accompany Brenda to the Christmas party. He would talk to some of the staff and their partners whilst slowly getting himself drunk. Ted was a quiet drunk and when he drank too much he would find the nearest chair flop into it and fall asleep. Brenda would have to ask some of the younger male staff to help her get him in a taxi at the end of the night. However, Ted did not want to go this year and had made some excuse about wanting to watch some programme on TV he had been looking forward to. Normally Brenda would have made some kind of protest and even suggested he tape this on the VCR recorder she had bought him a few Christmases ago, but tonight she did not say anything to him. Brenda ensured that Ted had everything he needed before getting dressed and leaving the house. Brenda had made an extra effort tonight and when she had gone into the living room to say goodbye to Ted, he failed to recognise or even notice how she looked and for a moment she had felt a pang of disappointment.

The party was already in full swing when Brenda arrived. The music was blaring out songs from the likes of Slade, Sister Sledge, David Bowie and Mick Jagger to name but a few and some of the younger staff were already drunk. Brenda noticed that Sue was already flirting with one of the projectionists as well as the other doormen.

Tracey had been quietly talking into the ear of Anton who

seemed to be staring at Reama the whole time. Brenda wondered if Anton was having a fling with Tracey. Like many others, she had also heard rumours that he had been with quite a few of the other girls and was working his way around. She looked around the room and as usual Edna was a no show. Brenda let out a deep sigh. She had tried years ago to encourage Edna to go out with her and some of the other girls but she had always flatly refused. Despite this for some reason Brenda had a liking for Edna and felt that if things were different and she was not so shy and retiring; they might have been great friends. Brenda did not really know that much about Edna who very rarely spoke about her own background and Brenda suspected that Edna did not have a happy childhood. She scanned the room and saw Sylvia who was standing alone in the corner. She had a glass of cherry Brandy in her hand and looked miserable as usual.

Brenda could not understand why Sylvia came to these functions. She was mean, nasty tempered and did not engage well with any of the staff. She had known Sylvia for many years and in that time, she had not changed one bit.

She had worn a black dress with long sleeves which came to her bony knees, her hair was in a beehive and the grey started to show through and needed another black dye on it. Sylvia had on a bright red lipstick and black eye liner. Sylvia never spoke about her past life and Brenda suspected that something horrible must have happened to her to explain why she behaved like she did. As if she knew she was thinking about her, Sylvia turned and looked straight at Brenda before walking off.

As Brenda continued to scan the room, she was not aware that someone had come up from behind her, put their arms around her waist and whispered, "You look absolutely amazing Brenda, I really mean that". It was Bill. Brenda stood motionless for a moment and felt her face starting to blush. She thought to herself that she was glad she had made the effort tonight and that she had decided to wear the red dress she had not initially been sure about.

She had even matched this with red shoes and a red bag with gold pearl drop earrings, matching necklace and bracelet. The colour had really bought out her eyes and

Brenda knew she looked good. She also now realised she had made this much effort just for Bill.

"Thanks Bill, I scrubbed up well right?"

"Brenda, love you could be wearing a black bin liner and still look amazing to me" Brenda felt herself blush even more.

The rest of the evening was spent in a dream. Bill stayed by her side all night, leaving occasionally to top her glass up with her favourite red wine. Bill had entertained and made Brenda laugh all night and she was glad that Ted had decided not to come after all. When the mistletoe started to make its way around, Brenda was not all surprised when Bill had held it over her head and leaned in for a kiss.

Brenda was more than happy to kiss him back and the kiss was something she had never ever experienced before; causing shock waves through her entire body. Brenda pulled back and stumbled after feeling lightheaded, but Bill had held onto her tightly. Brenda wondered for a brief moment whether she had drunk too much wine, but deep down she knew it was Bill and the way he had kissed her that made her feel like that. More than that Brenda had felt a stirring between her legs she had not felt in a very long time, so she excused herself quickly and rushed towards the bathroom. Once in the toilets, Brenda took a deep breath in and exhaled slowly. She walked towards the bathroom mirrors, took a hard look at herself and tried to talk herself back into reality.

"What are you playing at Brenda?, you're a grown married woman for goodness sake"! But she did not care. All she knew was that she wanted Bill with a passion she had never known before. As Brenda left the bathroom, she was not all that surprised to find Bill waiting for her. Before she could say anything, Bill had taken her into his arms and started to kiss her once more before taking her hand and leading her back into the bathroom inside a cubicle and locking the door.

The next morning, Brenda had lain awake in bed re-running the previous night's events over and over in her head. I had sex with Bill, I had sex with Bill, in the bloody toilets! Brenda could not believe what she had done. She would have loved to have blamed it on too much red wine but she had remembered every single detail of the night, of her actions and knew she was a willing sober participant. Bill had made her feel alive with passion and pleasure. He had ignited feelings in Brenda that she had buried deep inside for years and she had wanted Bill just as much as he had wanted her. They had ended up having sex twice before they were disturbed by someone coming into the bathroom and vomiting into one of the toilets. Whilst they were waiting for the person to leave, Brenda wondered if it was Elaine in there as she had heard her vomiting a few times before.

Brenda was worried about Elaine and what she was doing to herself but in the end it had turned out to be Sue who was the worse for wear. When Sue had left, Brenda and Bill slipped out of the bathroom as discreetly as they could and when they reached the corridor, they both began giggling and laughing like two naughty school children. Bill had told Brenda that he wanted to see her again to which she had eagerly agreed to before they headed back into the party. Bill had then spent the rest of the evening smiling and winking at her. Brenda knew she should feel worse than she did but she did not. She had always been faithful to Ted and as far as she knew he had been faithful to her but she had missed having sex and the intimacy that went with it. Brenda and Ted had not had sex in years and even though she still loved Ted, she no longer desired him nor was she physically attracted to him; not like how she felt about Bill. Bill made her feel young and alive again and she knew she did not want that feeling to end.

Chapter 12: Affairs of the heart

It had been two years since their affair had started and Bill was more in love with Brenda than ever before. Bill would have compared his relationship with Brenda to that of Burton and Taylor but without the glitz and the glamour!.

In short Bill had fallen hopelessly in love with Brenda and wanted nothing more than to be with her full time. He could not understand why she stayed with her husband. He knew they had slept in separate rooms for years and that they no longer had a sexual relationship, surely it would be easier for her to leave him? But Bill knew that Brenda loved and adored her family and in many ways was very loyal to them. He knew that her children were both grown up and living their own lives, then the grandchildren had come along, and Brenda adored and doted on them.

Brenda was the only woman ever to understand who he really was. She was smart, funny and he could talk to her for hours and hours without ever getting bored. Most of all she still looked pretty amazing to him and he could not understand for the life of him why her husband took her for granted and no longer saw what he saw. He had to be crazy! Nonetheless Bill wanted to be with Brenda and one day marry her. He had never in his life felt like this before. Their affair had been kept low key and as far as he was aware not many people knew about them. They were caught once by Anton when they were coming out of the stock room and they had sworn him to secrecy.

Bill chuckled to himself when he remembered the look on Anton's face when the penny had dropped as to what they had been doing. Anton had gone so red with embarrassment and was lost for words; instead he just nodded in agreement to what they had asked. It was not only the youth that could have a good time he thought to himself chuckling.

Anton did not mention this incident again and Bill had been grateful for that. Bill liked Anton and was glad it had been him and not any of the others who had caught them. He knew Anton had a bit of a reputation for being a ladies man and that it was rumoured that he was working his way through the younger female staff. Anton loved the ladies who in turn loved him back.

Anton himself had told Bill about some of the many women he had been with. He had also confided in him about a special someone who he had his eye on who he saw as more than just a conquest and who had not yet given into his advances. Bill also knew that Anton had been in a relationship but that this had fizzled out a while ago. Bill realised now why he liked Anton so much; he reminded him of how he would have liked to have been in his youth with all the confidence, arrogance and big talk. Anton may have been a lot better looking than his younger self, but Bill also had the type of look the girls seemed to gravitate towards.

Bill brought his thoughts back into the present. He was planning on meeting Brenda later on and they would be spending a rare night together at a local hotel. When these special occasions came about, Bill would pull out all the stops to make it a special evening; ensuring that he booked a nice hotel insisting that the room be filled with Brenda's favourite flowers and wine. He was really looking forward to tonight.

Brenda was sitting at a hospital bed holding Ted's pale looking hand. She had been crying silently to herself and the tears had made her make up run down her cheeks. There was no way she would be able to meet Bill later, not under these circumstances and she had no way of contacting him either. Ted had suffered a heart attack earlier in the morning. He had been in the bathroom at the time when he had fallen hitting his head on the sink basin which required several stitches.

Brenda's room was next door and she had been lying in bed thinking about meeting up with Bill later that evening when she heard a thump. She had called out to Ted a few times before she realised that something was wrong then fear began to take a hold of her. She had jumped out of bed and rushed to the bathroom where she had found Ted lying unconscious on the floor and blood gushing out of an open wound on the side of his head. She had run down the stairs and called for an ambulance all the time hoping that he would be ok. She had got herself ready in time before the ambulance arrived and took them both to hospital.

The journey there was the longest ride in her life as she watched the paramedics do their work on him. Once Ted had got to the hospital he was still unconscious and the Doctors had also become increasingly concerned about the injury to his head; Ted had swelling to his brain and the doctors said they would have to operate to reduce the swelling. Owing to his heart, they had been reluctant to operate straight away so they had put Ted in an induced coma.

Brenda knew she should feel guilty and ashamed of herself, but she had really been looking forward to tonight with Bill. It was very rare they got to spend the night together and this chance came about when some of the girls at work planned an overnight shopping trip to London. She had told Ted she wanted to go with them and he did not even question this. If she had told Ted she was flying to space he would have reacted in exactly the same way.

Brenda looked at Ted as he laid there and she suddenly felt

scared. What if Ted died? That thought had not crossed her mind until now. What would she do without him? She had been with Ted for most of her life and even though she no longer loved him like she used to; she still cared deeply for him. Once again the tears began to trickle down her face and she began silently crying again. A few hours later, the Doctors had come into the room to say it was time for them to operate on Ted.

Bill had been waiting in reception at the hotel for over three hours and a deep panic started to creep in. This was so unlike Brenda, who was always on time and Bill did not know what to do. He knew he was unable to call Brenda's home as this was strictly a no go zone. Any arrangements they made were done at work. If one person was not on shift, they would leave a note in the other's locker in the staff room. This type of communication had also added to the excitement of their relationship and the secrecy; but Bill was at a loss right now. He knew instinctively that something was really wrong but he did not know with whom.

Whilst Ted was in theatre, Brenda wondered how she could get in contact with Bill to let him know what had happened. Apart from Anton, the only other person to officially know about her and Bill was Reama. Brenda had been training Reama in how to stock take and how to manage the bar area and they had become quite close. Brenda had grown quite fond of her despite their age differences. Brenda had craved giving some maternal attention and had been pleased and appreciative that Reama did not mind when she did this. Over the weeks and months, Reama had started to confide in Brenda who had always been there with a listening ear.

Reama had also spoken to Brenda about her true feelings for Anton and her reluctance to get involved with him owing to his appalling womanising reputation. Reama had not been a hundred percent sure of how genuine his feelings towards her were and she was adamant she would not be another notch on his bedpost and Brenda could see where she was coming from.

One afternoon Brenda had come back late from break. She

had gone to meet Bill and they had lost track of the time and decided to have a quickie in the stock room. When she had rushed back, she had been all hot and flustered which never went unnoticed with Reama who had asked her directly if she had been having sex with Bill. At first Brenda was going to deny it but had actually felt relieved at having the opportunity to tell someone. So, she had told Reama everything on the understanding that she kept this to herself.

Brenda knew that Reama was not going to London with the other girls and had agreed to work some overtime as Brenda knew she was saving for a holiday. Brenda went to the Nurses bay and asked if she could use the phone. She dialled the office at Uptown Cinema and asked to be put through to the kiosk where Reama answered the phone.

"Hi Reama, its Brenda"

"Hi Brenda, what's up?"

"Ted's had a heart attack. When he collapsed in the bathroom he also hit his head on the sink which caused swelling to his brain. He is currently in surgery"

"Oh my God Brenda, will he be ok?"

"I hope so, they are doing everything they can and they are optimistic about this"

"How are you doing?"

"I feel sick, Reama. Earlier on, I had this horrible thought about Ted dying and what I would do without him. He has been a big part of my life for such a long time"

"I know Brenda, but you have to try and stay strong"

"I know"

"Oh my god, does Bill know?"

"No, that's why I'm calling you. He is waiting for me at the Smith Hotel in Town. I bet he's sat there thinking something terrible has happened and is probably worrying out of his mind. Could you call the hotel and let him know what has happened please? He should be waiting in reception"

"Of course I will. Do your kids know about their dad?"

"Yes, I called them earlier on. They are on their way here. I told them not to come straight away until I knew what was happening. Because his heart stabilised, they needed to operate to get the swelling down from his brain. I couldn't avoid them coming in the end"

"Ok"

"Thanks Reama, I really appreciate this"

"No worries Brenda, I'll let Bill know as soon as possible.

Brenda hung up the phone and made her way back to the family waiting room. An hour later she was joined by her children and their partners.

Bill had been grateful of the call he received from Reama. He had been waiting in reception for nearly four hours and people began to eye him suspiciously. He was stuck and had no clue what to do. The young receptionist had caught his eye and had beckoned him over to the front desk. She had asked him his name and when he had confirmed it was Bill and that he had been waiting for someone called Brenda she had handed him the phone. Bill's heart was pounding as he put the phone to his ear not knowing what to expect. When he heard Reama's voice he had been bitterly disappointed but had also been gripped with fear that something had happened to Brenda. Reama had quickly explained the situation to Bill who had felt relieved and still worried at the same time; relieved that it was not Brenda who was in danger but worried about what would happen to Ted.

For a fleeting moment Bill thought selfishly that if Ted were to die he could finally have Brenda all to himself but he quickly became ashamed of this thought and put it out of his mind. No he would just have to wait this out to see what would happen next. He really loved Brenda and believed she was worth the wait.

Chapter 13: Falling for you

Although Reama had felt an immediate attraction to Anton, she tried to dispel this, because she knew this was stepping in dangerous waters. She knew he was in a relationship with someone and had even met her on the odd occasion. This was when Anton felt he needed to remind people, as well as himself, that he was actually in a relationship.

Anton had chased every bit of skirt that he could whether they were staff or customers. Since he started working at Uptown Cinema he had been rumoured to have slept with at least six of the girls and that was in the first year.

Despite this, Anton had never chased Reama the same way that he did the others and always treated her differently and with more respect. He had asked her out on occasions, but she had always refused knowing what his reputation was. But somehow they had become good friends and Reama had been one of the few people who knew about his private life and him looking after his mum. This was the Anton she had liked and respected, the person she would eventually fall in love with. Reama remembered the first time she had kissed Anton at the staff Christmas party. They had both been drunk and the mistletoe had been passed around. When it had finally reached them, Anton had pointed out that she could not refuse the traditional kiss under the mistletoe. Before she could respond, he had reached down and kissed her without a care of who could be watching them.

Reama had been surprised at the way she had responded to Anton. His kiss had been soft and gentle at first and when she responded back to him it became much deeper and he began exploring her tongue as well as her lips. He had drawn her in closer to him and had tightened his grip around her. His kiss had caused such a physical reaction, her head had started spinning and she had felt light headed. The kiss felt like it would never stop until they were abruptly interrupted by a very drunken Tracey who insisted it was now her turn to be kissed under the mistletoe.

Reama was sure that Tracey had looked upset and even jealous but had quickly put this down to her drunken state.

Neither had said anything and for a moment they had just stared at each other before Anton left the party.

"What's up with him? Was it something that I said?" Tracey asked.

Reama never responded and went to get a drink giving her time to process what had just happened between them.

It was another week before she would see Anton again. In that time she had been asked a thousand questions by some of the girls about what they had seen. Reama noted that Tracey had been more than inquisitive about that and had asked her if she felt Anton had a thing for her. Reama did not know what to say so in the end she had just put it down to having too much to drink and being in a festive mood, but Tracey did not seem satisfied by this.

Anton was already at work when she had arrived, and he had barely said hello to her, avoiding any eye contact. As the day went on Anton tried to avoid Reama as much as he could until they found themselves on the same break. Anton had been sitting at the table staff used to eat their lunches, with his legs crossed eating a packet of biscuits.

Reama wondered how he could eat so much and never put on weight. Anton was always eating junk food, yet it never seemed to affect him. Reama had envied this as she had to go to the gym twice a week just to maintain her figure.

"Are you ok?" She asked.

"I am fine, why?"

"Because you have been avoiding me since I got here this morning"

"Well I have been busy!" His tone was sharp and hurtful.

"What's up Anton?"

"Nothing"

"It's not nothing and you damn well know it!"

"I'm fine Reama, honest"

"Is it your mum? is she ok?"

"My Mum is fine!"

"So, what is it?"

There was a long silence before Anton answered

"You!!"

"Me?"

"Yes you"

"What have I done?"

"Why won't you go out with me?"

"You know why!"

"No I don't"

"Anton, whatever it is that you have going on you clearly need to get it out of your system but I will not be another notch on your bedpost, you can forget that!"

"You wouldn't be would you? You are different"

"Really?" "how?"

"You just are. I feel I can talk to you about anything you're one of very few people that know about my mum and about my life"

"I'm not sure Anton"

"Why not?"

"Aren't you seeing Tracey?"

Silence.

"Well are you?"

"Yes, sort of, how did you know?"

"She's been asking me a lot of questions about that kiss and about us. I think she is in love with you".

Anton let out a loud groan, "Arrgh no!"

"This is what I'm talking about Anton, when are you going to stop messing about with these girls? Ever since you and Isabelle split up you've been like a dog in heat!"

Anton started to laugh.

"You have a way with words, Reama which is one of the many things I like about you!".

"Or maybe it's the fact that I won't just jump into bed with you!"

"Why not?"

"For the last time you know why not. I also suggest that you set the record straight with Tracey"

"I know I know I'll do it later; I'm supposed to be seeing her tonight. If I do that then will you go out with me? even if it's just for a meal?

"I'll think about it."

"Please Reama just one meal?"

"I said I'll think about it"

"Well, that's something!"

Anton grabbed the last few biscuits from the packet and left the room.

There was no doubt in her mind that Reama liked Anton and found him physically attractive. She just struggled to get past his reputation and how some of the girls swooned and talked about him. Reama had never gotten involved with their banter and had always kept her own counsel about her feelings towards him. This, along with the fact that she was terrified he would use her like he used the others. She knew that he treated her differently from the others and had more respect for her but still she worried. He confided in her about his family and having to take care of his mother, he had even told her how he had felt when his father had left.

Reama suspected Anton's behaviour had something to do with his father leaving and had even challenged him about this which he denied of course. However, Reama was certain about one thing; she was falling in love with him. Anton had left the staff room with a glimmer of hope and tried not to smile too widely to himself. The thought of even taking Reama out for a meal had sent his stomach into a flurry of flips and somersaults.

Anton was absolutely in love with Reama and now started to believe she felt the same way too, he could feel it. He re-called for the hundredth time the night they kissed and how he had held onto her. He had never felt such a strong desire before. He had got lost in their kiss and had entered a world where dreams actually came true before they were rudely interrupted by Tracey!

In the last few weeks Tracey was beginning to irritate and annoy him, and he knew it was time to call it a day with her. She had by far been the most creative person he ever had sex with, and she had not shied away from any of the suggestions he made to her, but this was where it ended. He did not care for Tracey, but he had noticed that she was becoming clingy, more demanding of his time and showing signs of jealousy. Her behaviour the other night was just an example of this. He reflected back to the Christmas party and remembered that he had been so taken aback by that kiss he had felt he needed to get out and have time to think. Anton had wanted Reama in a way he had never wanted anyone else and it was starting to drive him crazy.

When he first started dating Isabelle, their sex life had been great and they could not get enough of each other. Isabelle was living with him at the time, but she later moved into a place of her own. Their sex life had continued to be great until Anton's mum had a setback and he needed to spend more time with her. His mum had been admitted to hospital but after a few days she had begged him to take her home. Anton had been reluctant at first but eventually he gave in and agreed. The more time he spent with his mum meant less time spent with Isabelle and over time she became less and less tolerant of his caring responsibilities.

On one of the rare nights they spent together, they had a massive argument about him caring for his mum and he stormed out of the house. Anton remembered he had gone to a local pub and whilst there he had met someone he knew from school. They started talking about old times and in the end she invited him back to her place and he did not object.

When Anton had sex, it allowed him to block out and forget the pressures he felt under, allowing him to focus on pleasing the woman lying underneath him. The act of having sex made him feel powerful and in control and he never wanted the feeling to end. This one night stand soon became the start of a pattern of behaviour that would not be so easy to break. A few months later it was no surprise that he and Isabelle had split up for good.

Anton met up with Tracey later that night. When he arrived at her flat she had met him at the door wearing a sexy black basque, stockings, suspender belt and high heel shoes; she looked stunning. He quickly averted his gaze away from her and walking past her went straight into the room. He knew this would not be easy.

"Tracey we need to talk"

"About what?"

"Me and you"

Anton could see the change in Tracey as he looked at her. All of a sudden she became self-conscious and had gone into the bedroom to get a dressing gown which she quickly wrapped around herself.

"What is it Anton"?

"I can't do this any more Tracey, it has to stop"

"Why?"

"Because it does, I've had enough"

Tracey had started to pace the floor with her arms folded.

"But I love you Anton, I thought you loved me too"

"No, I don't Tracey, I thought you always understood that this was never serious between us, it was just fun".

"It wasn't just fun for me. Is there someone else?"

Silence.

"Well?"

"That is none of your concern!"

Tracey had started to cry, and tears slowly trickled down her face. She threw herself towards Anton and tried to put her arms around him, but he pushed her away.

"Is it Reama?" she asked.

Silence

"I know it's her, I see the way you look at her. You have never looked at me like that, never!"

"I'm sorry, Tracey"

"Like hell you are! You used me"

Anton did not know what to say. He did like Tracey and the times they shared together. They could have a laugh and joke and really got on, but he did not care for her the way he cared for Reama. It was sexual between them that's all. Out of the blue Tracey had launched herself at him again hitting out at him with her fists.

"You used me, you used me!"

Anton had to use his strength to pull her off him, pushing her to one side before storming out of the flat.

As much as he wanted to see her, Anton decided to leave Reama alone for the next few days. Tracey had not turned up for work and he had felt it was for the best. He still felt badly about ending things with Tracey but his feelings for Reama were stronger.

It was about a week later whilst on shift together that he got the opportunity to speak with Reama. She had been in the kiosk speaking with Brenda and wondered what they were talking about. He had felt strangely nervous but decided that he would speak with her the next opportunity they got. When things had died down and films were playing he had gone up to her at the kiosk.

"It's over between me and Tracey".

"I know".

"How did you know"

"Sue told me. Tracey is very upset. She is not eating or sleeping. Heartbroken apparently".

"I'm sorry that Tracey feels that way, but it had to be done.

I want to be with you. So, can I take you out?"

Reama was quiet for a while. She had felt sorry for Tracey when Sue had told her what happened and even a bit guilty but knew Anton had done the right thing. It had been difficult not seeing or speaking to him since it happened, but she felt it was the best thing to do. She knew that if she went out with Anton, even for a meal it would devastate Tracey, and this is what she had pondered on.

"Yes, you can, but we can't tell anyone yet".

Anton was so happy that she agreed he did not care that they had to keep it a secret from everyone. They had arranged to go out later that week for a meal and had such a wonderful time. They saw each other again the next day and then the next and were soon seeing each other as often as possible. They had found that they had really enjoyed each other's company and had a lot in common. Anton did not rush things sexually with Reama, preferring to wait as long as possible. A few weeks later, they went to a club in a nearby town and had a brilliant time. The music was nice, and the drinks were flowing. Anton and Reama had kept their eyes locked on each other the entire night kissing and cuddling, at times forgetting they were in a club. As the night drew close Anton suggested that they leave.

They got a taxi and when they reached Reama's house; she did not want the night to end so they went on to Anton's. He knew his mum would be fast asleep as he had ensured she had taken her medication and settled for the night. As they got to the front door he began kissing her with such eagerness. He had taken her by the hand and led her up the stairs towards his room.

In the bedroom they continued kissing. Anton opened Reama's blouse slowly, twisting each button with his thumb and third finger, then running his finger along her breastbone. When her shirt finally fell open, he studied her, then caressed her breasts. He gently laid her down on his bed, licked her nipples, then moved his lips slowly down her stomach.

Anton removed Reama's underwear and kissing her just above her pubic bone, he slipped two fingers inside her.

Reama moved into his hands until he stopped suddenly, removing his fingers as if he had thought better of the whole thing. Reama closed her eyes, feeling his lips on the side of her neck, feeling his fingers tracing the length of her thigh. There came the pressure of a warm hand clasping her down below, fingers slipping inside her again, lips against her lips. Fingers pinched her nipples hurtfully and deliciously... She felt herself being lifted, her body no longer touched the bed, the darkness swirled around her, strong hands turned her, and stroked her all over. She felt his strength increasing and let out a gasp. She was floating in the air. She reached up to him, groping in the shadowy tangle of arms supporting her, felt her legs coming apart and her mouth opened. He entered her slowly and they made love for the first time. He kissed her until she arched her body to meet him once more and they fell asleep in sweet exhaustion.

A while later and naked now, Anton laid his full length over her. She enjoyed his weight on her and enjoyed being crushed under his body. She wanted him fused to her, from mouth to feet. Shivers passed through her body. Reama knew she was in love with him.

Chapter 14: Anton and Reama

Reama was looking forward to their weekend getaway. She felt it would also give her the opportunity to speak with Anton. He had seemed distant from her since she told him she had been offered a place in London on a journalism course to start in September. She remembered that she had been so excited to share her news with him. At first he had seemed really happy for her, but over time he began to engage in less conversations with her about it and had started to withdraw seeing him less than usual.

They had arranged to spend the weekend at Norwood Hall. Anton had a friend who worked there and they were able to go for a decent price.

Reama had never been to Norwood Hall before and it was such a beautiful place. It was set in twenty six acres of spectacular grounds with a combination of period properties with modern facilities. It boosted over a hundred rooms which were all thoughtfully furnished to create a relaxing environment.

The room they were given was a king size suite. As they entered the room there was a large king size bed which seemed to take over the entire room. The bed was so big Reama believed it would hold at least four people comfortably. On either side of the bed was a small oak cabinet with one drawer with a lamp sat on each. Opposite the bed was an oak dressing table with three drawers on either side and a chair sat in between.

On the table was a silver tray housing a small silver teapot with two cups and a silver bowl offering an array of sugars, teas, coffees and dried milk. Next to this was a coffee machine which doubled up as the kettle, Reama had never seen anything like this before.

The carpet was deep blue in colour with curtains to match which spanned the entire length of the wall masking the largest windows she had ever seen. It was the most magnificent room Reama had ever been in.

The bathroom was just as beautiful. There was a large bath which housed a shower with a shower curtain to one side.

The towels, when she touched them, felt soft and fluffy; towels never felt like this growing up at home.

Reama was impressed as to the lengths Anton had gone to, to make this weekend special. She had been so busy admiring the room, that she did not notice how quiet Anton had been.

"Oh Anton, it's beautiful. Thank You so much for this"

"I'm glad you like it". Reama noticed that Anton was not fully present.

"Anton, what's the matter? don't you like the room?"

"Of course I do"

"So, what's wrong? you don't seem that impressed or interested for that matter?"

"I am okay, I just have a lot on my mind"

"Is it your mum? Are you worried about her?"

"I am always worried about my mum"

"So, what else is it?"

"It's nothing"

Anton had been sitting on the bed so Reama went and sat next to him.

"Of course something is wrong Anton, you have been more

distant with me for a few weeks now and we have hardly been talking. I know something is up"

Anton, held Reama's hand and looked at her.

"I am going to miss you when you leave"

"I will miss you too Anton"

" Reama, I don't want you to go. Stay here with me, please"

Reama was stunned to hear what Anton had said. She believed they had talked about this and agreed she would be going.

"What?, Anton we have talked about this, that's not a fair thing to say. You know I have been wanting to do that course for such a long time!"

"I know, but why London? Why do you have to go all the way there?"

"Anton, you know why, we have talked about this, loads of times. It offers the best course in the country and once I graduate, I am more likely to get into what I want to do. You know I want to be a writer and all the best opportunities are in London".

"I know, but I can't help the way I feel. You know I would

come with you but it's my mum".

"I know Anton, I understand, but the course won't be for long and we can visit each other as often as we can".

"Huh, I don't know".

"What do you mean, you don't know? This is what we agreed to, what we planned to do!"

" I know, but you will forget all about me once you get there. You will be so busy with your course and meeting and socialising with new friends, meeting other guys.... You won't find time for me"

Anton knew that what he was saying was unfair and childish, but he was unable to help himself. He had really fallen in love with Reama and had never felt this way about anyone in his life. He simply was not ready to let her go. When Reama had got the offer to go to London, Anton was thrilled for her but deep down he had hoped that she would not get accepted. He knew it was selfish to think like that, as it would mean a new life for Reama whilst his own life stayed the same. Anton felt trapped sometimes and wished he could escape himself. Since she told him he had been thinking a lot about his own life and what it had become, and it was not what he had planned it to be. Anton loved his mum more than anything in the world, but he did not imagine that he would have ended up being her main carer. His mum's condition had deteriorated, and he had all but given up his job to take care of her. He still did the odd shift which he looked forward to as this was his break away from his day to day caring responsibilities. Anton had often felt that he was somehow holding Reama back and had been feeling this way a lot more over the last few weeks. He knew he could not hold her back and that she needed to follow her dreams, but what were his? He had been pondering this a lot. He was smart and did well at school and at college and if he put his mind to it, he could probably do most things, but fate had other plans. He could not and would not abandon his mum, but he also knew it would be unfair to keep Reama in his life.

He knew she would spend every penny she had to come back and visit him, give up the opportunity to go out with her new friends to sit and listen to how his day was spent, washing and feeding his mum, the amount of incontinence pants she was going through, how many times that day she fell out of bed, how much medication she was taking and the endless list of chores he had to do. No, this was not fair on Reama who he knew deserved a lot more than this, than what he could give her. That is why he made a decision about the future, a decision he knew would hurt them both. They unpacked their cases and decided to go for a walk before heading off to the restaurant.

At Norwood Hall, visitors could enjoy the peace and quiet of the gardens with its scented flowers and fountain which looked beautiful in the spring displaying an array of bluebells and daffodils. Reama loved springtime. She loved the aroma of spring and how it percolated through the air. As they walked, she inhaled deeply and the potpourri of scents which registered as a sweet mix of jasmine, grass and blossoms tickled her nose. She could hear buzzing bees surf the open spaces from flower to flower, desperately seeking pollen.

At the end of the large grounds there was a grove of trees. Apple trees ran through the centre of the garden, casting a lake of claw like shadows onto the grass. Further down the grounds there was a river which had a magical quality to it that Reama had not seen elsewhere. The water was so clear she could easily spot the speckled goldfish at the bottom. Beyond that there was a plush-green meadow which stretched away into the hills. Reama could see why people believed that romance was richly suited to this place.

They walked further through the immaculate grounds and finally sat on a nearby bench, watching the sun slowly rise over the hills in the distance. Its full splendour revealed itself and soaked the garden with the brightness of its smile. A blackbird descended from the air onto a nearby branch and launched into a beautiful solo song. It was a welcome invasion of the mounting awkwardness between Reama and Anton.

They made their way to the plush restaurant situated at the back of the Hall overlooking the gardens. It was huge with oak tables and furnished with velvet red cushioned chairs. Chandeliers lined the vast ceilings to give out light and ambience to the room which was very charming and pleasing to the eye.

As they sat down to order, Reama noticed that Anton looked tired. He had not said much since they left the room and wondered if his mum's health was getting worse. Reama admired Anton so much for the dedication and commitment he showed. He had given up a lot to care for his mum and this was one of the things she loved about him. She knew there was no way he would come with her to London and she understood this, so she was even more determined to make things work between them. Reama was really in love with Anton but knew if she stayed, she would always regret this. It was a great opportunity for her, and there was no way she would let it pass her by. Writing was her dream and something she had wanted to do for as long as she could remember.

Anton also knew this and he had believed in her and supported her dream, but what he had said earlier had really unnerved her. He had never spoken to her like that before and she had been taken by surprise. They had ordered some wine and she noted that Anton was drinking slightly more than usual. They ordered their meal which was steak and chips but Reama suddenly lost her appetite.

"Anton, are you sure you're okay?"

"Yes, I am fine."

Anton realised that the mood had changed between them and knew this was unfair. He had already decided that this would be their last time together and he had to make it special for Reama, she at least deserved that. Anton changed the subject to talk about Brenda and Bill and how things were going between them.

After Brenda's husband got out of the hospital she had remained by his side and nursed him back to full health. She had not seen Bill for a few months who had been going out of his mind with jealousy. Bill had spoken to Anton at length about his feelings for Brenda and said he felt unable to live without her. In the end Brenda chose Ted. His near-death experience had made her realise that she still loved him and their family and she knew they would all be devastated (and disappointed) if they ever learned of her affair.

In the end Bill had left Uptown Cinema. The thought of

seeing Brenda every day was too much for him. Anton still heard from him now and again and he had moved to a nearby town and had taken a job at its local cinema. Reama was glad for the change of topic as the mood lifted. They continued in idle chat before heading back to their room.

When they got back into the room Anton pulled Reama into his arms and started to kiss her. Reama wanted to kiss Anton forever. She blocked out all thoughts about London and what it was going to mean. Reama had kissed Anton until reason seeped out through her pores and she became a living pulse, conscious only of the love she felt for him in that moment. Oh, God, she thought, the scent and taste and feel of him. It was like tiny fireworks going off all over her body, reigniting her back to life.

During the course of their relationship, they had lots of sex, but tonight was really special and once again, Anton proved his ability to keep Reama drunk from his love. They just had another amazing night of deep, slow lovemaking and Reama's heart felt like it could burst. The entire time they were wrapped up tight in each other's arms, with Anton deep inside Reama, thrusting ever so slowly and every once in a while. It was the deepest sex Reama had ever experienced, so deep it hurt a little at one point. But it was so special, and Anton was so gentle with her. As they held each other tight, they whispered I love you to each other over and over, hugging each other tighter with each profession of their love. Running her fingers through his hair, whilst he held her in the tightest embrace Reama had ever felt. He whispered loving words in her ear; they were in their own little heaven, pulling back to look into each other's eyes and just staring at each other and smiling.

Reama broke out into a smile when she looked at him and thought, he is my entire world. Anton had said the sweetest, most loving things to her tonight. She had felt so overwhelmed by his love that she cried happy tears into his shoulder as he cradled her in his arms before they again made love extra slow.

Chapter 15: Love hurts

The weekend flew by so quickly. During the day they would take a walk through the vast grounds taking in the picturesque scenery before them and at night they would make sweet love. Nothing felt better than the way they melted together when they made love, the way their two hearts become one.

Reama marvelled at the way she still got crazy butterflies whenever Anton gave her that look, and she knew instinctively when it was about to happen. His kiss still made her melt in his arms and when he looked her in the eyes and smiled at her the way he did; it still made her blush.

Reama felt that what they had was truly a gift and she felt so blessed and lucky to have a love like this. Making love with Anton was the most beautiful, pure, loving experience Reama had ever known. Little did Reama know that the weekend would turn out to be both magical and devastating, all at the same time.

As the weekend drew to a close, once again, Reama had noted a change in Anton's behaviour. Anton had been so quiet and subdued and he barely looked at Reama. She instinctively knew it had something to do with her going away.

In the morning before they left, they had gone for a walk and had sat on a bench by the lake taking in the early morning sun. Little rays of sunshine were glistening in the lake like shards of glass. They could hear the sounds of the birds singing in the air and the occasional barking of a dog pierced the deafening silence developing between them.

Anton knew that time was running out. He knew that if he did not take action now, it would make matters worse. He had thought this through a million times and believed he was doing the right thing. He had to let Reama go. Anton took Reama's hand and looked her in the eyes.

"Reama, I think we should split up"

For a minute Reama thought she had mis-heard what he had said.

"What?"

"I think we should end things, this is not going to work for me"

Reama was dumbfounded.

"What are you saying Anton?, I don't understand?"

"It's over Reama. As I said before, if you're going to have such a great time in London, you won't have time to see me. You'll be too busy with college and making new friends. I know you will make the effort to come and see me, but eventually you will resent coming up to see me"

Tears began to roll down Anton's cheeks. He knew he was breaking her heart, but his heart was breaking too, he had to do this.

"I don't get it, I thought we sorted this out? I don't mind coming back my family are here too"

"I know"

"Don't you love me anymore?"

"Of course I do Reama, but I know I just can't do this. You know me, I'll end up straying anyway!"

"You don't mean that"

"It is who I am Reama"

"Not anymore, you've changed. Have you been faithful to me the whole time we have been together?"

"Of course I have, but you won't be here will you?"

Reama was speechless. Why was Anton saying this to her? She knew he had not been himself lately and that he did not want her to go but he understood this was important to her.

"I am sorry Reama"

"Are you Anton?"

Reama felt numb, then a wall of tears began to build behind her eyes. Her nose started to burn and her throat started to get tight. Her hands were clasped together so tight, her knuckles turned white as she started to shake.

Looking back, she remembered the thoughts of denial swirling round her head. No, no, no this cannot be happening, he does not mean it, he is just upset, we will sort it out. Suddenly Reama's stomach dropped as if she were on a roller coaster ride. Her mouth started to water, and she felt unable to breathe. Her nose became clogged and her face felt wet. No matter how hard she tried to speak, the words would not come out.

She had learned to trust Anton with all her heart and she

had been happy. Anton made her feel alive and now it was gone. She looked at Anton, unable to comprehend that this had been the same person who had made love to her that very same morning. If hearts could shatter into a million pieces, then hers did just that. She wanted to beg him to change his mind but knew instinctively that this would not have made a difference.

The old Anton was back. Reama got up from the bench and without saying another word and still in a blur, she returned to the room, packed her bags and called for a taxi to pick her up. In all that time, Anton never once came to the room to ask her to stay, that he was sorry and wanted to take back what he had said. Reama broke down crying on the bed. Later that night at home Reama had still felt in shock. She had been laying on her bed trying to make sense of what had happened whilst trying to navigate her feelings of panic, anger and pain. She had been comprehending the idea that those moments on the bench at Norwood Hall would be the last time she would ever see Anton, her heart had been broken.

Anton had no idea how long he had remained on that bench after Reama had gone. He had to use all of his strength and will power not to chase after her and tell her he had not meant what he said, beg her forgiveness for being so cruel but he did not, he could not. His body felt numb and he felt an emptiness in the pit of his stomach. He knew he had done the right thing and as he reflected on their time together, he began to sob.

After her breakup from Anton, Reama had initially taken this as a feeling of rejection, and heartbreak. She had not spoken to Anton since leaving Norwood Hall and he refused to answer her calls. She struggled to sleep, found it difficult to eat and could not stop vomiting. Her parents had been so worried about her, they had called a doctor. After a few weeks, she made the heart-breaking decision to move sooner than she had planned to London. Although it was difficult, her parents had been very supportive of her decision. Her mum particularly had told her to follow her dream and that she would do everything she could to ensure she realised this and would take care of everything. Reama had arranged to stay with relatives who had said it was ok for her to come earlier.

Before heading for the train station, she had resisted the urge to go and see Anton. She wanted so desperately to speak with him and wanted to tell him. But she knew deep down in her heart that it was for the best. She knew he had ended things for her sake but it still hurt like hell.

After a few weeks, Reama channelled all her energy into doing things that would make her feel better. She had gone to the theatre and had visited all the places she had promised herself she would do.

Reama thought about Anton every day for months after they broke up, particularly at the times she had come back to visit her family. These visits were difficult enough as she missed them so much and every time she left; she felt her heart break all over again. There were many times when she had to stop herself from calling him especially when his mum had died. She had heard about her death through Sue, whom she had the occasional contact with. When they talked, Sue never talked about Anton but when his mum died, she had to let her know.

Reama had been really upset to hear the news and the first thing she wanted to do was get on a train and go straight to him, to comfort him in his grief but she held back. The thought of seeing him again would be too much. She still felt a rawness inside and knew her heart would break all over again if she saw him.

There had been no one else in her life since they broke up. Over time she had forced herself to go on dates, but her head and heart just was not into it and she would never return for a second date. She immersed herself in her course and then her work and it was then she started to write, which led to her first book being published. Over time and little by little her heart started to mend.

Within a few years Reama had formed a great group of friends that she could not imagine her life without, a new job that was setting her up for a legit career, and she eventually found how to be happy by herself.

Anton had felt a deep peace in being able to give Reama the freedom to take whatever path she wanted in life. He knew that if he had tried to hold on to her she would have probably stayed but he needed her to value him and not stick around just out of a sense of duty. For Anton it had been a total sacrifice, an act of compassion and generosity.

During their relationship, Anton had been so 'in love' and comfortable with what he had, that he did not push himself to actually achieve any dreams of his own and create his own personal happiness. His mum had needed him too much and he had dropped out of University to care for her.

After his mum had died, he had felt so alone and even though he knew she was dying, her death had broken him. The funeral was small and not many people had attended. His dad had showed up, but Anton had refused to speak to him. After all the years he had become a stranger to him. He wanted to reach out to Reama so much but thought the better of it. She had a new life now and he hoped that she was happy, but he had missed her so much, her touch, her smell, her smile, the way she laughed. He had gone out and bought every one of her books and he had been so proud of her which made the decision to let her go more tolerable. He missed everything about her and not a day went by where he did not think about her.

After his mum's funeral, life had pulled Anton in different directions, had introduced him to new people, and had given him a completely new perspective. Over the years he focused on bettering himself, building a strong career that would serve as the foundation for the life he would have, but more importantly, rebuilding a part of himself that was once lost. He had been in and out of relationships and had dated someone for six months, but Anton could not find anyone to fill the void he felt inside.

But Anton lived, hoping that one day something amazing would happen; something that would make sense of everything he had sacrificed and been through.

Epilogue

As Reama walked out to meet her audience, she had no clue as to how many people would be there to see her. Right at the front were some familiar faces from Uptown Cinema, cheering her along, but there was one familiar face she could not see amongst the sea of faces. Was he going to be there?

She could hear the original Uptown Cinema theme tune playing in the background as she moved towards the audience to shake hands and sign her books. She looked up and saw her name in glittering lights and that sense of achievement overwhelmed her and burst her with pride. She had done well, success was all she had dreamed about and now she really was living the dream.

She had money, a beautiful apartment and friends from all over the world but deep down she knew she did not have the love she so desired; the love of someone special who had captured her heart all those years ago.

A lot had happened in that time and through Facebook Reama had kept the occasional contact with some of the girls. She had heard that Edna had died from a heart attack and Sylvia was in an old people's home. As she scanned the crowd, she spotted Elaine and smiled and nodded at her. Elaine had two children, now a girl and a boy. She had been married briefly but this had broken down due to her continued use of amphetamines in a bid to keep her weight down. Even from a distance she still looked painfully thin.

Reama spotted Sue in the crowd and saw that she was with her girlfriend Louise, looking really happy. She had heard once that Sue had declared her love to Tracey many years back and this did not go down very well with Tracey who eventually broke off their friendship. They had not seen each other in years.

After this rejection, Sue had decided to come out to everyone who had been surprised but never treated her any differently. Sue had been in and out of relationships since then and could never quite find anyone to replace how she felt about Tracey until she had met Louise. Reama wondered again if she would see him and her stomach flipped butterflies at the thought.

Reama did not see Tracey but was not surprised. After she had found out about her and Anton, she had stopped talking to her. She had heard that Tracey was still single. She had a child and Reama had no knowledge about the child's father or what had happened between them.

After Brenda refused to leave her husband and Bill left Uptown Cinema, Reama later learned that Bill had turned to alcohol and in later life died from cirrhosis of the liver. When Brenda learned of his death, it had devastated her and she never really recovered from this, eventually dying herself eighteen months later from a heart attack.

Reama started thinking about what ever happened to Mr Langley and Mrs Cross when she looked up across the crowd and saw her family. She could see her sisters, her dad and her mum and was about to wave at them when suddenly her heart skipped a beat. He had come. There standing by her mum, tall and handsome as she remembered and looking just like his father, was her son.

Printed in Great Britain
by Amazon

76964844R00119